MARS BORN

SHADOWS OF THE VOID BOOK 8

J.J. GREEN

INFINITEBOOK

BOOKS ORDER

The Books of Shadows of the Void - Complete Series

Prequel: Starbound
Book 1: Generation
Book 2: Stranded
Book 3: Dawn
Book 4: Shadowrise
Book 5: Underworld
Book 6: Burned
Book 7: Trapped
Book 8: Mars Born
Book 9: Shadow Battle
Book 10: Shadow War
Books 1 - 3 The Galathea Chronicles
Books 4 - 7 The Earth Chronicles
Books 8 - 10 The Galactic Chronicles

1

Jas went through her training moves. Left jab. Right jab. Right kick. Spin. Left kick. Weave. Right hook. Left hook. Weave. Right kick. She'd made something that vaguely resembled a punching bag from a rolled and taped up bunk mat, and she'd hung it from the ceiling in the starship's dining room. It was the only place on board that was large enough for her to train in. Between meals, she would detach the tables and benches from the floor and stack them against the walls before starting long exercise sessions.

The center of the punching bag contained a long plastic bag filled with water, but the bag wasn't quite heavy enough, and it swung wildly at Jas's last, low kick. She side-stepped as the bag swung back, and she kicked it again, hard, as it passed her. On its second return she punched the bag, grunting with the effort. The bag swung away again, and as it came back, she stepped up to meet it and began jabbing it with increasingly fast blows.

Her brow glistened and her breath came in soft pants. Her arms and legs ached and her knuckles and wrists were sore, but she didn't want to stop. The exercise felt good, though no matter how fast or hard she punched and kicked, the effort didn't dispel her feelings of frustration.

Letting loose something between a gasp and a cry, she jabbed hard with her right fist. A soft pop followed, and water gushed from the bottom of the bag, drenching her feet.

"Krat," she exclaimed, backing away from the quickly spreading puddle. The punching bag swung like a pendulum, shedding water like an out-of-control fire hose.

Carl Lingiari was sitting on the floor in the corner of the room, concentrating on an interface he'd balanced on his knees. "Whoa," he said as he heard Jas's exclamation and saw the spilling water. He scrambled to his feet. "Must have been some punch, Jas," he said, his eyebrows raised.

Her feet had been soaked in the initial burst of water, so she gave up trying to avoid it. She stood in the puddle, her hands on her hips, watching the slowly swinging bag. She drew her arm across her forehead to wipe off the sweat. "No, not really. The plastic bag was too weak. Wish I had some proper training equipment." Pulling off the surgical tape she'd wrapped around her knuckles, she went over to Carl, her feet squishing in her wet sneakers. "What are you doing?" she asked as she trod on the heels of her shoes to remove them. She bent down to pull off her socks.

"Just the usual," Carl replied. "Checking to see if there's been any mention of the Shadows in the media. Isn't it about time you gave the training a rest? You've been going at it a couple of hours now, and you were in here all morning too, weren't you?"

Gazing down at her red, battered knuckles and lifting one lip ruefully, Jas replied, "Yeah, maybe you're right. It's just that I don't have anything else to do. It's so boring here.

We've been aboard this ship for three days. Three days. And we can't seem to decide anything. Every discussion we have goes around in circles. We're all cooped up on this starship talking, and meanwhile the Shadows are on Earth killing more and more people, replacing them with replicants, taking over the Government, companies, media, everything." She wrung out her socks over the puddle in the center of the room. "If we don't do something soon, I think I'm going to explode."

"Hard to know what to do until we hear from the Transgalactic Council."

"I know. I know now that the Lees' house is destroyed, any reply from the Council is going to be lost. And I know that we have no idea who Sayen's parents sent the message to." She squeezed her eyes shut in frustration. "I get it. But knowing all that doesn't make things any easier. We have to decide something, and soon. Or else we might as well say we've done our part and wash our hands of the whole problem. Just find ourselves a little corner of the galaxy to wait out the storm, and hope that if we ever return to Earth, it isn't inhabited by Shadows."

"After what's happened over the last few months," Carl said, "that part about finding a quiet corner of the galaxy doesn't sound so crazy. 'Cept I'd just want to pick up Flux first and say goodbye to my old home."

Jas's heart ached at her friend's words. She couldn't imagine what it was like to know your parents had been killed by Shadows. She reached out to softly touch Carl's upper arm. "Whatever we do, we'll pick up Flux. We'll insist on it."

"Yeah. Little fella'll be wondering where I've got to."

They stood quietly for a moment. Jas didn't remove her hand from her friend's arm. They both lifted their eyes and their gaze met. Slowly, they leaned closer. Jas closed her eyes and froze. She was trying to force her way through a sickening dread and not turn away or stop what might be about to happen, to not freeze Carl out as she had done so many times before.

At that second the door opened, and Phelan Lee peered around it.

"Oh, sorry," he said, backing out.

"No, it's fine," said Jas as she hastily drew back from Carl, avoiding his wounded look. Relief eased her churning stomach. "What is it?"

"We're having a meeting." Phelan eyed the puddle in the middle of the dining room. He went to a small hatch in the center of the floor and pushed it down with his foot. The hatch popped open, revealing a floor drain. The water flowed away. "I thought you two would want to come along."

"You bet we would," Jas said, too brightly.

THEY FOLLOWED Phelan toward the bridge. Jas was still getting used to how much he resembled his sister. Though the two were three years apart in age, it was as if they were male and female versions of the same person. Both looked a lot like their mother.

Phelan was anatomically flawless as his sister, Sayen, no doubt due to the state-of-the-art genetic modding he'd received soon after his conception. The man's physical proportions were exactly balanced, and his face was perfectly symmetrical. His blond hair was even cut to a similar cropped style as his sister's. His personality, however, was quite different.

"Hope I wasn't disturbing anything back there," he said,

throwing a grin over his shoulder. “But, you know, there’s more comfortable places for that kind of thing than a soggy canteen.”

“No worries,” Carl replied, “you weren’t disturbing anything.”

Jas winced at the somber tone of his remark.

Phelan seemed to pick up that he was skirting the edges of a touchy subject. “So,” he continued, “can I ask, was there a special reason you wanted to flood my crew’s dining area, Jas?”

“Sorry about that,” she replied and went on to explain about the makeshift punching bag and the accident.

“You went to all that trouble just to make yourself some training equipment?” Phelan asked.

“Yeah, I did. There’s nothing aboard. I like to stay in shape, and I wanted to pass the time. I hope that was okay. I’ll unroll the mat. It should dry out in a few hours.”

“Yeahhhh,” Phelan said, drawing out the word. “The mat’s no problem. I was only wondering why, if you wanted something to train with, you didn’t just use the ship’s printer.”

Jas nearly drew to a halt at her own stupidity. Of course Phelan had a printer on board. Every starship she’d worked on had carried a printer to create essential items or spare parts for repairs in an emergency. But because they were expensive to run, printers were locked away. Crew members were only allowed to use them with special permission. It hadn’t occurred to her to ask Phelan if he had a printer. “Krat. That was kind of dumb of me, wasn’t it?”

“Kinda.” Phelan gave a short laugh. “Just kidding. You couldn’t have been expected to know that, I guess. But for the record, you can use whatever the crew use aboard my ship. No need to ask. You're friends of my sis, and what's mine's yours, okay? I should've made that clearer sooner."

"Thanks, that's generous of you," Carl said. "How's Sayen doing?"

Phelan had fallen into step beside them. The three walking abreast took up all the room in the narrow corridor. Space was at a premium aboard Phelan's mining ship, the *Bricoleur*.

Sadness dimmed the man's usually bright features. "Not so good. My parents' deaths have hit her pretty hard. She was very close to them both, especially to our mother. Sayen hasn't said so, but I think she's so cut up because, when it came down to it, Mama chose our daddy over us. I think that hurts her almost more than the fact that they're gone."

Reminded of the scene of their escape from the Shadows on the burning rooftop, Jas shuddered. The noise and heat of the flames, the sight of Mr. Lee bravely firing at the host of aliens speeding toward them, and Mrs. Lee pushing Phelan into the shuttle, forcing them to flee and leave the couple to their fate: these were things she'd never forget.

2

The bridge was the second largest room aboard the mining ship, aside from the equipment bay and the hold. Phelan sat in his captain's seat, throwing a baseball from hand to hand, as he always did when he was thinking. The crew and guests ranged around the space, standing or sitting where a spare seat was available.

Jas wondered if Phelan had excelled at the ancient sport of baseball as he and Sayen had no doubt done at most things while they were growing up. He threw the ball at the ceiling and caught it on the rebound. At the place where the ball had hit was a smudge of dirt, evidence of the captain's long habit. She wondered if the practice irritated his crew as much as it did her.

It was hard to tell. No one, apart from Phelan and the pilot was human. The whole company was there, from the lowliest miner to the second-in-command and engineer, Flahive. Everyone was looking bored after three days of inactivity. Everyone except Flahive. It was hard to tell how the engineer was feeling because he—if his species consisted of hes and shes—was encased head-to-toe in a pressure suit. Flahive came from a high-g planet, and if he didn't remain inside the suit, his entire body would rapidly expand, eventually killing him.

Flahive's suit gave an indication of his species' tripoidal anatomy. He had three stumpy legs and got around by jumping along on the foremost two while the rear leg kept balance. Carl had said he reminded him of a 'roo'. Flahive's three upper limbs were equally spaced around his torso, about halfway between his legs and dome-like head. At the end of each upper limb was a highly flexible pad, and the alien could manipulate the one at the back just as easily as the two that were closer to his front, as he was demonstrating at that moment by working on the interface on the panel behind him. What his face looked like, Jas had no idea, for it was hidden behind a smoky panel.

The miners were all one species. Hairy and cylindrical, they stood about half Jas's height. They didn't appear to have any method of holding or touching anything, and Jas had never figured out how they worked the mining equipment. She supposed they had some kind of retractable appendages.

The ship's navigator was an android similar to the servants of the Lees' household. She acted and sounded human, but Jas had guessed what she was from her extremely deferential attitude and limited conversational ability. The android was also extremely attractive, and it had crossed Jas's mind that navigation wasn't the only reason Phelan had her on the crew list.

Sayen had propped herself on the edge of an instrument panel as they were waiting to begin the meeting. Her face was pale and her head low. Makey was peering over the pilot's shoulder at levels she was adjusting on her screen. A young woman, the pilot was very reserved and quiet and had rarely contributed anything to the discussions they'd had on what to do next.

Thunk went Phelan's baseball on the ceiling of the bridge. On the rebound, it slapped into his palm. As he went to throw it again, Jas resisted the urge to snatch it in midair, run to the nearest airlock, throw it in, and press Purge.

They were waiting on Erielle, the crippled underworlder. It felt like an age ago since Jas had first met her, though it was only a few weeks.

The bridge was crowded, and Jas wondered why Phelan had decided to hold the meeting there rather than the larger dining room. Maybe he was about to make a big decision, and he needed his spot on the ceiling.

The bridge doors slid apart, and Erielle walked through. Jas sat up in surprise. The underworlder had been getting around on crutches since her legs had suffered severe laser burns, but she'd replaced them with a frame of slim metal rods that encased her from her waist to her ankles.

"Looking good," Phelan said to the underworlder. "It worked then?"

"Yeah. Thanks for the suggestion, hun. I really appreciate it. Hey, everyone, what do you think of my new leg supports?" For the first time in weeks, Erielle smiled.

Sayen looked up, and her face brightened momentarily. "You look sneck. Did you print them?"

Erielle nodded. "Your brother suggested it. My legs are still kratted, and they always will be unless I get them fixed, but with these supports I can walk normally. I can even run. And I'm a little more comfortable."

Makey went over to the underworlder and squatted down to inspect the metal scaffolding around her legs. "Wow. I bet these make you stronger than you were before."

He straightened up and turned to Phelan. "Can I have some too?"

A general laugh echoed around the bridge. Phelan shrugged. "I don't see why—"

"How about you concentrate on getting your body into shape first?" Jas interjected. At Makey's crestfallen look, she added, "Supports are great for helping people with problems, but they don't match the flexibility or responsiveness of natural legs. You wouldn't want to be wearing leg augmentation in a fight. Am I right?" she asked Phelan.

"She's got a point, kid," Phelan replied. "Though if you were running away..." He paused at Jas's frown and gave a chuckle.

Carl stood up to give Erielle his seat, and as the older woman sat down, Phelan cleared his throat. "Okay, we all know why we're here. We've argued it out, we've thought about it, we've argued some more. We aren't getting anywhere. Some of you think we should skedaddle back to the Outer Rim and carry on like nothing's happened." The miners fidgeted and mumbled. "Some of you want to return to Earth and start rooting out these Shadows wherever we can find them."

"That's right," Erielle said forcefully.

"Though it isn't clear how you'll tell who's a Shadow and who isn't since this scanner you've told me about went up in flames," Phelan said.

"We'll figure out a way," said Erielle. "People are dying down there."

"And if we return to Earth we'll likely die too," Sayen said. "There has to be something more useful we can do. If we can just contact the Council...whoever received my parents' message packet must have informed the rest of them. They must—"

"As I've said all along, the Transgalactic Council must receive a million messages a day from crazies all around the galaxy," said Erielle. "Why would—"

"No." Sayen rubbed her tired-looking eyes. "My parents had connections at the Council, and we sent them the evidence."

"You *think* you sent them the evidence," Erielle said.

"We sent them the evidence," Sayen replied with an edge in her voice. "Not everyone in authority is out to get you, Erielle. If we can't trust the Council to help us, who can we trust?"

Erielle opened her mouth to speak, but Flahive cut in. "Please, if you both don't calm down I'll have to ask for a minute's silence and reflection." The voice his comm unit generated was male, deep, and smooth. As always happened when the alien spoke, soft lights illuminated his face plate. Flahive had given the same warning at every discussion they'd had when things had gotten heated. Jas hadn't yet figured out why, but Phelan never reacted or seemed to think there was anything out of the ordinary about it.

Thunk. The captain caught his ball and tossed it from one hand to the other. "Listen up, folks. I'm gonna lay it on the line for y'all. Here's my problem. I have a duty to my sis and her friends, I have a duty to my crew, and I have a duty to the good citizens of Earth. Only thing is, all my duties aren't lining up. I can't help one of you without hurting the other. If I help Sayen, I'll be taking my crew into danger. If I try to keep y'all safe by hiding out somewhere until this all blows over, I'm neglecting to help my fellow human beings, and that isn't right.

"So, after listening to all your arguments, I'm gonna act like the captain of this ship that I am and make up all your minds for you. Or, leastways, I'm gonna make a decision and y'all can decide which way you're gonna jump.

"I'm not comfortable sitting here in orbit above our infested home planet. If these Shadows' reach stretches as far as you tell me, and as it sounds like they're especially keen to find you, they might figure out who I have on board soon enough. The *Bricoleur* isn't a combat ship. We won't be winning any space battles. So we need to move, and soon. But where to go? The Council's spread across the galaxy. We don't know where my parents sent their message, so until we figure out who we should be talking to, we can't go to the Council yet. It seems to me the logical thing to do is to sit tight while we try to find out what's happening."

"But if it isn't safe to stay in orbit above Earth..." said Jas.

"I didn't mean to stay right here, like a duck waiting to be shot. We only need to stay in the vicinity. Somewhere close by. Somewhere hopefully not infested with Shadows yet."

"I get it," Makey exclaimed. "We're going to Mars, aren't we?"

3

Phelan's plan was to cancel the contracts of anyone in the crew who wanted out and shuttle them to Earth or Mars as they desired. Everyone had been mulling about the problem for days, and it didn't take them long to state their wishes. The pilot said she wanted to return to Earth and check on her family, and she hoped that would be okay now that Carl was there to fly the ship. Carl was happy to take over the position. He only asked that he could first make a quick trip to his family home to pick up his alien friend, Flux.

The miners were disgruntled about Phelan's decision to halt his mining operations. They didn't want to go to Earth or Mars, nor have their contracts canceled early. Phelan listened to their protests, throwing and catching his baseball the entire time.

Finally, he offered to pay early termination bonuses and to provide them with tickets from Mars to their home planet. After putting their hairy heads together and talking in their strange, buzzing language, they reluctantly agreed.

They filed out, muttering among themselves like a crowd of angry wasps. The pilot followed.

Flahive said he wanted to stay on, providing that Sayen and Erielle could sort out their differences. It turned out that the point was moot because, avoiding Sayen's teary gaze, Erielle asked to be set down in the Shadow-infested state capital that had long been her home. At Erielle's words Sayen said nothing, but stalked from the room, her head bowed and her lips set.

The underworlder rested her chin on her hand and sighed. The older woman's hair had grown out from the buzz cut she'd worn when Jas had first met her. The effect softened her hard features a little, though the suffering and pain she'd endured ever since she'd been dragged into the battle with the Shadows was still evident in her face.

"I know what you're all thinking," Erielle said. "If I go back to Earth, it'll be a suicide mission. But they're my people down there. All their lives they've been shunned and despised for not being modded, or for not conforming to the system. Ignored. Rejected. When the Shadows make their move, and it comes to a fight, who's going to be looking out for them? No one. They might not be pretty, and they might not be smart, and most of them sure as hell aren't trustworthy or responsible, but I spent all my life trying to help them. I'm not going to abandon them just because that's the easy thing to do."

"I can see why Sis likes you so much," Phelan said. "You're a brave woman."

Erielle smiled grimly. "Not brave. Just resigned."

"It's going to be hard on Sayen," said Jas.

"I know. I must seem like a callous bitch. Believe me, I don't want to put her through any more pain so close to her parents dying. I don't mean to hurt her. I know it might not look like it sometimes, but she means a lot to me. I'll go talk to her."

"I'm coming with you," Makey said.

"You're coming with me to talk to Sayen?"

"No, I'm returning to Earth too."

"What?" exclaimed Jas. "No. No way."

"Yes, I am. You can't tell me what to do with my life. I'm not a kid anymore. I can do what I like."

"You can't go, Makey," Jas said. "It's insane. You'll get killed."

"It's like Erielle says. People on Earth need our help. We can't just forget about them."

"We aren't forgetting about them. We're doing everything we can to help them. Sacrificing yourself isn't going to help anyone."

"I won't be sacrificing myself. I'll be with Erielle, and we'll help keep each other safe. She always wanted me to join the underworlders, and she's right. Everyone on Dawn was an underworlder. I owe it to my mam and sister to help them."

He sighed. "It's funny. All my life I dreamed of escaping my home planet and traveling the galaxy. And maybe I'll do that one day. But I couldn't look at myself in a mirror without shame if I ran away from the Shadows again like I did on Dawn. Don't get me wrong. I'm grateful you helped me, Jas and Carl, but if I'm honest, a day hasn't passed that I didn't regret leaving. Everything I've done has been to try to make amends for what I did. It's not enough. I have to go back to Earth and continue the fight against the Shadows there. I'm sorry, but it's just the right thing for me to do."

With a tiny metallic hiss from her leg supports, Erielle got up and went out. Makey went with her. Only Phelan, Carl, Jas, the android, and Flahive remained.

"I'll program a jump to Mars," the android said and turned her slim, shapely back to them as she bent over her screen.

"I'm hoping the Shadows haven't arrived there yet," Phelan said. "We need to restock on supplies, so we have to go planetside. What do you think, Jas? Is it likely to be safe? Have you been back recently?"

Jas rubbed her eyes, trying to get the image of Makey being dragged into a Shadow trap out of her mind. "I haven't been back since I was twelve years old. I made it as far as orbit once, but that's it."

Phelan whistled. "Not been back since you were twelve years old, huh?" *Thunk.*

A muscle in Jas's jaw twitched.

"I sense you're extremely worried about Makey, Jas, and very conflicted about returning to the place of your birth," said Flahive. "Perhaps it might help you to go to Mars as a way of examining your feelings and achieving a resolution to them."

"I'm sorry?" Jas said. "You sense I'm...*what*?"

"Flahive." Phelan gave the engineer a little shake of his head.

"Ah, that was inappropriate of me," Flahive said. "I apologize, Jas. I'm very sorry. I was just trying to help."

A look of puzzlement passed between Carl and Jas. The engineer's opaque face plate was enigmatic.

Phelan sighed. "I guess now that we're all going to be shipmates for the duration, I should tell you about Flahive. Or do you want to tell them yourself?" he asked the engineer.

"I find it best if I do the explaining, Captain, if you don't mind. It's certainly not the first time, and I doubt it'll be the last that I have to reassure other species about my ability."

Why would they need reassurance? Jas wondered. She didn't think she was going to like what the alien had to say.

"Firstly," Flahive said, "I want to make it very clear that I cannot read human minds."

Jas had been right. She didn't like the sound of where Flahive seemed to be heading with his explanation.

He went on, "However, I do pick up on strong emotions. Not everyday, minor feelings of contentment, annoyance, dissatisfaction, that kind of thing. But joy, elation, despair, hatred, love, passion, fury, those I can sense. I sense a kind of echo of them. At times, the effect is quite uncomfortable."

The alien's objections when Sayen and Erielle had fought began to make sense. He was an empath.

"I know this can make some humans feel self-conscious or embarrassed, but I've never truly comprehended why. Strong emotions can be an opportunity to initiate much-needed change. They aren't something to be avoided or hidden away. Sometimes emotions bring people together, or advance the individual to enlightenment of some kind. When I sense powerful feelings, I try to encourage an exploration of those feelings if I think it might help that person."

Oh, brother.

"Okay, I think you've explained enough," Phelan said. "Don't worry," he said to Jas and Carl. "You'll get used to him being around. You won't even think about it after a while. I don't." *Thunk.*

"I'll get used to him knowing exactly how I feel?" Jas spluttered. "All the time? He'll be picking up on our emotions all the time we're aboard the ship? Or are you limited by distance?" she asked Flahive.

"My ability *is* limited by distance," Flahive replied.

Jas made a mental note to stay as far away from the alien as she could.

"But it stretches as far as the confines of this ship."

"Great," Jas said.

Phelan gave a short laugh. "Calm down. It isn't a big deal."

"Yes, you should probably calm down," Flahive repeated.

"Don't tell me how I should feel," exclaimed Jas. But Carl was laughing at her now.

"Besides," continued Phelan. "We need Flahive. If something goes wrong with the engine, he's the only one who can talk to it."

Carl's laughter died. "He can *what?*"

4

They were in Mars orbit. The *Bricoleur* was quieter with Erielle, Makey, the pilot, and the miners gone. Four days had passed since the last of them had left. Flux's addition to the crew had caused a temporary lifting of the spirits, but the atmosphere had quickly returned to a subdued and pensive state.

Carl was the only person aboard who had been planet-side, but he hadn't stuck around. He'd remained at Valles Marineris Spaceport just long enough for the miners to disembark the shuttle before flying back.

He was worried about Sayen. After Erielle had left them, her mood had sunk even lower. She was rarely seen outside her cabin, and she ate very little at meals—when she turned up to them at all. She'd grown worryingly thin, and her eyes were shadowed in their sockets. Her depression was bringing her brother down too. Phelan spent most of his time with her, though when the two were seen together he would be the one doing the talking. He would reason with her, or go over stories of their childhood, or just generally try to cheer her up. His naturally buoyant temperament was less and less evident as time wore on.

Carl decided to pay her a visit and take Flux with him in the hopes that the quirky alien's presence might lighten her mood. He rang her door chime twice before she answered, and when she opened her door it was evident she'd been crying. "I'm sorry, Carl. This isn't a good—"

Flux took off from Carl's shoulder and flew into her cabin, alighting on the corner of her bunk.

"Got anything to eat?" the creature asked, his Australian-accented voice high-pitched.

"No, Flux. I don't have anything. Maybe you should try the dining room?"

"Nah, nothing good in there. How about I scout around for some cockroaches?" He flew down from her bunk and crawled underneath it, pulling himself forward with the hooks on his wings.

"There are no roaches in my cabin," Sayen exclaimed. Her cabin was extremely neat and tidy—almost too neat and tidy, as if no one were living there. The surfaces were completely bare and there wasn't a smudge or speck of dust in the place.

"I bet there are," came Flux's voice from under the bunk. "Y' can always find one if you look hard enough."

"Sorry about him," Carl said. "Is it okay if I come in, just for a minute?"

Sighing, Sayen stepped back to let Carl in. She told the door to close.

"Can I get you a drink?" she asked as she went to the dispenser on her wall.

"No, that's okay," Carl replied. As Sayen filled a beaker with water, he noticed that her hands were red and raw, as if she'd been washing them excessively.

Carl took the only chair in the cramped room, and Sayen sat on her bunk, her elbows on her knees and her head bowed. Scratching sounds were coming from beneath her bunk where Flux was searching.

Now that he was there, Carl wasn't sure what to say. *How are you doing* seemed trite.

Sayen broke the awkward silence. "Carl, I know why you're here, and I appreciate it and all, but there isn't anything you can say or do that's going to make me feel better. Phelan's tried his best, but he can't bring Mama or Daddy back, and now that Erielle's gone too..." She paused and swallowed. "It's like the light's gone out of my life, and there's nothing I or anyone else can do about it."

"Nothing under here," Flux said, crawling out from beneath Sayen's bunk. He climbed up the side and onto her mattress, gripping her blanket with his feet and wing hooks. "I'll try up there," he squeaked, launching himself into the air. He flew across the cabin to the top of a cupboard on the opposite wall and disappeared into the gap between it and the ceiling.

"There's no roaches there either," said Sayen.

"I wouldn't be too sure about that if I were you," came Flux's voice.

Carl rolled his eyes at Sayen and was pleased to see the corners of her lips twitch into a half smile, but the moment was soon over.

"Your brother seems to be coping pretty well, at least," he said.

Sayen shook her head. "He's hurting. He just won't show it. We aren't much alike in that way. He doesn't easily show how he feels. Mama and Daddy's choice of modding for him was a little too far on the tough and adventurous side, they always said. I think they overcompensated with me. Made me too emotional and timid."

"Maybe you were a little like that, at one time," Carl replied, remembering her as he'd first known her when she was navigator aboard the *Galathea*. "But that doesn't sound like the Sayen I know now. The Sayen who broke into the secret files the Government was keeping on Shadows wasn't emotional and timid. And neither was the Sayen who saved me and Makey after the truck crashed and we were surrounded." He would never forget that lasting image he had of her appearing on top of the flaming truck, herself in flames.

"Seems like a long time ago," said Sayen. "I was a different person then."

"It just shows, though, doesn't it? We aren't set in stone. People can change. Modding's only one part of who we are. We can still choose how we act and how we react when we hit hard times. We don't have to accept that's how we'll be forever."

Sayen frowned. "I guess so."

Flux flew down and landed on Carl's shoulder. "No luck," he said disappointedly. "You keep your cabin too clean," he said to Sayen.

"Er...sorry about that."

The creature began to pick through Carl's hair.

"You're not going to find anything in there either, mate," Carl said, brushing away a curl that had flopped over one eye.

"You never know," Flux replied, leaning in to peer at Carl's scalp.

This brought a small chuckle from Sayen. Carl thought he would take advantage of the momentary break in her mood with a change of subject. “Hey, did you know about the *Bricoleur’s* engine?” he asked.

“The Oootoon drive? Yeah, I know about it. Phelan had to argue long and hard with our parents about buying the ship when they were loaning him the money to start up his business. They didn’t think the greater efficiency of an Oootoon engine was worth the necessity of always having an empath aboard.”

“So it’s true that the engine’s alive and can communicate?”

“Oh yes. You could talk to it too, if you wanted to. You have to open the engine casing and touch it. I did it once, when the ship was delivered.” She grimaced. “What’s inside doesn’t look like much. It’s just a thick yellow liquid, but I wouldn’t recommend touching it. You immediately hear all its thoughts, and it’s like being inside the head of someone with multiple personality disorder. Confusing and creepy.” She gave a slight shudder. “Took me a little while to get over it.”

“Right...why does the engine need an empath?”

“An Oootoon drive will take you wherever you tell it, in hops like a starjump engine, only it’s a fraction of the size and it doesn’t need any fuel. The last I heard, no one’s figured out how it does it. But if the engine’s damaged or something upsets it, you have to have a way of talking to it, or it might stop working. Like I said, talking to it isn’t easy, but empaths like Flahive can do it. Flahive doesn’t need to touch the Oootoon to communicate with it. And he doesn’t just feel its emotions like with us; he can hear what it’s saying if he ‘tunes in’, as he puts it.”

“Wow,” Carl said. “I’ve never heard of anything like it.”

“Humans are still on the fringes of galactic society. We’ve only had interstellar travel for a couple of hundred years, whereas some alien species have been exploring the galaxy for eons. We've barely touched the surface of what's out there. You should hear some of the stories Phelan has to tell about what he's seen and done."

"Sounds like I should. Ow." Carl frowned and looked up from beneath his brows at Flux, who had just pulled his hair.

"Sorry, mate," the creature said. "Thought I saw something."

Carl gently removed the animal from his shoulder. "Maybe you should give it a rest for a minute," he said, sitting Flux on his knee.

"Yeah. A rest sounds like a good idea." Flux climbed over Carl's lap and pulled open the top of Carl's shirt before climbing in, saying, "You two carry on. Don't mind about me."

Flux made himself comfortable inside Carl's shirt. Carl winced as his friend's claws tugged at his chest hairs. Holding open the top of his shirt, he peered inside. Flux had curled into a ball and wrapped himself in his transparent wings. In a moment, his eyes began to close and his mouth opened, revealing two rows of tiny, sharp teeth. The creature's breathing became deeper and more regular.

"It's good to have him back," he said to Sayen quietly, "but I'd forgotten how much of a pain in the arse he can be."

"I can hear you," Flux said.

Carl smiled at Sayen, and she grinned back.

5

Jas fastened her safety belt, breathed in and exhaled slowly as Carl piloted the shuttle away from the *Bricoleur*. Breathing deeply didn't do much to slow her racing heart. Thinking rationally, it made sense for her to be the one to go planetside. She was the only one with Martian citizenship, which meant that she could enter and move around in Mars Territory freely, providing she passed the health check at immigration. Her coloring also meant that she would blend in easily with the local population and remain relatively inconspicuous. She was the ideal person to assess the place for signs of Shadow infiltration.

On the other hand, if the Shadows had arrived on Mars and were looking for her, she could quickly find herself in hot water. But with Mars' much lower population, little deep space traffic, and far tighter controls on who entered and left, she didn't think it likely that the Shadows had penetrated its defenses.

Yet it wasn't fear of Shadows that was making Jas's stomach clench into knots as Carl flew her to Valles Marineris Spaceport. All her life she'd avoided dwelling on her childhood, which had begun on Mars. Her unknown parents' death had been the first in a series of experiences that had marred her early years.

After being forced to travel to Earth so her bones wouldn't be permanently weakened by Mars' low gravity, things had gone from bad to worse. Global Government policy at the time had mandated that Martian children were separated from their peers to better enable their integration into Earth society. The intention was good, but the effects were poor. Jas had been relentlessly bullied at her Earth institute for cared-for children. Then a traumatic experience while at training college in Antarctica had been the final straw.

Jas's past was a place she'd never wanted to return to, in word or deed, but here she was, traveling back in time as well as space.

"Touchdown in five," came Carl's voice over the passenger cabin speakers. Jas jumped a little as she was jolted out of her musings, surprised that so much time had passed so quickly.

She could have sat next to Carl in the co-pilot's seat, but he hadn't offered and she hadn't asked. He'd been a little cold toward her since that time in the dining room when they'd nearly kissed. She didn't blame him. He'd made his feelings clear and deep down, she reciprocated them. Yet she'd been acting like a nervous sixteen year old, moving ahead only to shy away as soon as anything at all serious began to happen.

What's wrong with me?

Jas shook her head slightly. She knew exactly what was wrong. What she didn't know was how to fix it.

It was night time in Valles Marineris, and the spaceport was a triangle of brilliant lights at one end of the valley.

Points of light ran out from the triangle, marking the overground tunnels of the Loop, which led to the colony settlements. Spreading patches of silver and red, they ran across the valley floor and up into the surrounding foothills.

The lights burned brighter as the shuttle vibrated and descended vertically to the landing pad. It came to rest outside a utilitarian, gray building with the words Valles Marineris Immigration Control stenciled across it in red.

The roar of the shuttle engines quietened, and the vibrations ceased. Jas undid her safety belt, but she hesitated, hoping for something before she disembarked. After a moment, her silent wish came true. The door to the cockpit opened and Carl's lanky frame filled it, leaning against the edge.

"All set?" he asked.

"Yep. Ready as I'll ever be." She got up and retrieved her bag from the locker.

"Remember," Carl said, "if you need to leave earlier than we arranged, just send the word. The *Bricoleur's* right above. I can be here in a couple of hours."

"I'll remember. Hopefully, it won't come to that."

"Yeah. Hopefully. Have you figured out where you're gonna go yet?"

"First, I'm going to find a place to stay. Then in the morning I thought I'd try to talk to the governor. See if there's been any comms from the Council. Maybe the Territory officials know about the Shadows already. It's a long shot, but it's worth a try."

"Hmm, yeah. Got any plans to go anywhere else?"

"You mean am I going to go back to the place where I grew up? Maybe. I haven't made up my mind yet. It's been so long, everyone I remember will have moved on."

"What about the colony?"

"The disaster site? No, I don't think I'll bother. They must have rebuilt it decades ago. I don't see any point in going there."

Carl looked doubtful, but he didn't say anything else. The pause began to turn awkward, so Jas shouldered her bag. "I'll be off."

"Okay."

Another pause. Jas wanted nothing more than to step over to Carl and hug him, but her feet wouldn't take her where her heart wanted to go. Instead, they turned her around and carried her to the exit.

"See you soon," she said over her shoulder, unable to meet his gaze.

"Yeah. See you soon. Good luck, Jas."

6

Dr. Sparks was a temperate man and rarely experienced extreme emotions, but after his long secondment investigating the Paths, he was nearing the end of his tether. The death of the administrator who had tried to cut them while they were aboard Polestar's satellite quarantine station had intensified the company's scrutiny of the creatures. Rather than releasing Sparks to his usual duty as medical officer aboard prospecting starships, Polestar had insisted that he accompany the Paths to their more specialized labs on Mars. Anything that could kill had potential to be a weapon, of course.

What Sparks didn't understand was why it had to be *him* doing the experimenting. Other Polestar scientific officers were better qualified and more experienced in research work. Three of them had been assigned to research the Paths alongside him: Graydon, Adrieux, and Rincker. Two women and one man with little to say outside of scientific discussions.

Sparks assumed it was a security issue. They were keeping him on task to limit his ability to divulge secrets. He wished he could air his sense of grievance about his secondment, but there never seemed to be an appropriate opportunity. Maybe they had an NDA to sign. He'd gladly do it for the opportunity to escape the research facility and return to what he did best: practicing medicine. But he never felt comfortable enough under their withering stares to express his dissatisfaction nor broach the subject of moving on.

When it came to the highly lucrative and explosive nature of weapons research, he also wasn't sure what Polestar was capable of doing in order to keep a discovery under wraps. It wasn't like he felt under threat day to day, but he knew the company was ruthless when it came to safeguarding its profits.

Each morning Sparks felt unsure that he could endure one more day of research on the cryptic Paths. Nothing he nor his colleagues had done had yielded quantifiable, statistically significant results beyond those he'd observed and recorded on the quarantine station. The odd, periodic *fading* of the creatures, the weird euphoric trance of the research assistant, Rogers, and the administrator's death remained unexplained.

All the researchers had managed to do was to induce either a temporary coma or death in animals that threatened the Paths. However, because the animals they'd used were dumb creatures incapable of vocalizing their experiences, no one was any wiser as to exactly *what* the Paths were doing or how they were doing it.

Sparks and his fellow scientists had recorded elevated heart rates, blood pressure, and brain activity of comatose animals, and the cessation of heart function in those that died. The simple difference between the Paths' response lay in the degree to which they felt threatened.

After yet another morning of boring, fruitless experimentation, Sparks was eating lunch with his colleagues. All four were intent on their interfaces as usual. The lack of meaningful conversation made alternative sources of entertainment necessary.

Sparks was reading about the recent appointment of a new Martian Governor. The man in question was a natural, and he made no effort to hide it. In fact, he was known for championing naturals' right to work and to freedom from discrimination. The politician had cited what Sparks believed to be flawed research. The studies supposedly demonstrated that natural selection was more likely than gene modding for high intelligence to give rise to geniuses like Einstein, Hawking, and Casson. Researchers proposed that humankind's understanding of the genetic foundation of intelligence was still incomplete, and that as yet poorly understood environmental factors could play a large role in the determination of intellectual ability.

The notion that random gene selection and upbringing could produce anything superior to sophisticated modding was preposterous to Sparks, and he unconsciously snorted in derision as he read the article.

Graydon noticed his reaction. A phlegmatic woman with a horsey face and long, lank hair, she'd always held an antipathy toward Sparks.

"Something funny?" she asked.

"Er, no, not really," Sparks replied.

"Hmpf," Graydon said and returned to her interface.

Ordinarily, Sparks would have left it at that. He knew his views on modded individuals versus naturals weren't politically correct, and over the years he'd become accustomed to being circumspect about to whom he aired them. He was sure that many others shared his opinion that genetic modification produced human beings who were superior in every way to their counterparts, but that few dared speak the truth about the matter. He'd learned to keep silent unless he was fairly sure he was speaking to a like-minded individual.

Today was different. Weeks of boredom and frustration made him careless.

"It's this new governor," he blurted, so loudly that all three of his colleagues took notice. "I mean, what were people thinking? Why has he been voted in? I don't understand it."

"What don't you understand?" asked Graydon. Her dark look should have warned Sparks to moderate his words, but he was intent on getting all his resentment and irritation off his chest.

"What I don't understand is, why would anyone elect a natural? I mean, what does a natural have to offer? Compared to someone whose parents actually *cared* about how their child turned out?"

Graydon put down her interface and folded her arms over her chest. Her eyes were hooded. Rincker was gesturing with his hand for Sparks to cut it out, but he took no notice.

"You think someone who was modded would do a better job as governor?" Graydon asked.

"Isn't it obvious?" Sparks replied. "Do I need to spell it out? Genetic modification creates better human beings. That's what it's *for*," he added, as if explaining to a child. "That's the whole point, isn't it?"

Sparks finally began to notice the woman's severe expression, and the weight of comprehension settled over his stomach. "Of course, not that *all* naturals are inferior. Only...only..." He swallowed. "Only some. I mean, it stands to reason, with the genetic variation involved in natural selection, that modification is required to avoid..." His words dried up and a flush crept from his neck to his face.

Rincker cleared his throat in the uncomfortable silence. Graydon carefully pushed back her chair and stood. Without a word, she left the table.

"Need I tell you?" Rincker asked Sparks.

"She's a natural." Sparks groaned and buried his face in his hands. After a moment he pressed his palms down on the table. "How was I to know? I mean, who could have guessed that someone in her position could have gotten where she is without modding?"

Rincker raised his eyebrows. "Don't you think you've said enough?"

Sparks clenched his jaw and returned to scrutinizing his interface, though he didn't register what was written on the screen. He was too preoccupied with his feeling of somehow being duped.

LATER, Sparks was sure that Graydon had something to do with the decision that came down from above to use one of 'their own' to test the Paths' threat response. It made no sense, of course. Scientists didn't experiment on themselves. They used volunteers or occasionally prisoners. But the word came, apparently, that as none of the animal tests had yielded useful results, a scientist was required to move the experimentation to the next level.

As the tests were top secret, the person had to be someone who was already involved in the study and understood the required observations. There was no drawing of straws. Sparks was told by the others that he would be the one to approach the Paths with a scalpel, as Rogers had on the quarantine station before falling into a coma.

In vain he'd searched his colleagues' faces for signs of

sympathy or concern for his well-being. Sure that any attempt to avoid the task would result in his incarceration, or worse, he had no choice but to agree. He only hoped that the Paths would induce the euphoric coma Rogers had experienced, and not their other response when under threat.

Brusquely, his colleagues attached electrodes to his chest, fingers and scalp. They would transmit data as the experiment took place. Sparks needed no readouts to tell him how his body was reacting. He was shaking and sweating so badly he could hardly hold the scalpel.

They placed a safety helmet over the scalp electrodes and pads to his knees and elbows to help prevent injury if he should collapse. In Sparks's opinion their efforts to help protect him were almost comical.

The Paths were in their sealed chamber. Weeks after their removal from the mysteriously buried starship on the hostile aliens' planet, they had survived miraculously with no food or water. As the scientists had discovered, they were apparently also unfazed by prolonged exposure to extreme temperatures and a vacuum.

Sparks gazed with hatred at the innocuous-looking, inverted, fungus-like bags. The creatures had caused him so much suffering, he would have gladly shoved the scalpel into them and cut them to shreds if it weren't for the fact that such an action would inevitably result in his death.

On Sparks's right, his colleagues were watching him through a thickened glass panel. Their faces were impassive. Sparks's rage rose up against his treatment as a test subject. *He* should be on the other side of the glass, patiently observing what was going on.

Graydon gestured at him. He scowled and took a step closer to the Paths. They remained predictably still, but

Sparks began to experience heightened sensations of panic and fear. Though he knew the feelings originated with the aliens, they felt very real to him.

What wouldn't he give to swap places with Graydon? It should be *her* in here, not him. He was modded. He was better. His life was *worth more.*

She was frowning at him and gesturing for him to move closer. She spoke, and Sparks lip-read, *Get on with it.* It was as much as he could do not to lift the scalpel and shake it at her—threaten her with it rather than the Paths.

If he got out of the chamber alive, he'd get his revenge. He'd make her pay. Flames of anger coursed through his veins. He would get the experiment over with. Turning back to the Paths, he strode toward them, almost running in his haste.

He didn't even feel his head hit the floor. He was in nirvana, and he never wanted to leave.

7

Jas put down her bag and went to look out the window of the viewing platform in her hotel room. The rocky Martian landscape spread out to the left beyond the distant spaceport. A shuttle was taking off, the brilliant glow of its rockets slowly fading as it forced its way up through the thin Martian atmosphere. On the right were the snaking lines of the hyperloop tunnels linking domes that marked the entrances to underground towns, factories, and farms. The small, pale sun was setting on the far side of the thinly spaced domes, and the sky was rapidly changing from pink to black as hard, white stars came out.

Mars hadn't changed much, from what Jas could remember. She wasn't surprised. A couple of decades wasn't long in the terraforming process. The modded soil bacteria that scientists had seeded the planet with were doing their job, but enriching Mars' atmosphere with sufficient oxygen to make it breathable would take centuries, if it were actually possible. Many doubted the planet could ever sustain an atmosphere anywhere near equivalent to Earth's.

Colonization had begun prior to the invention of interstellar flight, but it really took off when global warming had reached its peak and millions of refugees were fleeing famine, natural disasters, and ruined local environments. Richer countries closed their borders, and for many, Mars was the only escape.

Jas recalled what her dead Martian friend, Ozment, had told her: the planet had also provided a haven for those escaping increasing division in societies. Genetic modification had become the new privilege, but not all parents could afford the high cost of altering their offsprings' genes just after conception, or they had a philosophical objection to the process. Unmodded children tended to grow up poorer and more disadvantaged. Though the newly formed Global Government hadn't been slow to outlaw the requirement to reveal one's genetic status when applying for jobs or educational courses, modding generally produced smarter, more creative and sociable, physically enhanced individuals. Their advantages were clear, and *natural* became a slur.

Those who rejected the new social order, or who were rejected by it—underworlders—had come to Mars in droves.

In recent years, however, galactic colonization had taken off. Beyond the Solar System were planets far more favorable to life than Mars. The flood of new Martians had dried to a trickle, and then reversed, as they abandoned their cold, dry, barren world for friendlier planets. Jas wondered if Mars would eventually be entirely deserted, and the underground settlements would one day be as empty of life as the surface; if Valles Marineris and the rest of the municipalities dotted over the planet would become no more than ghost towns, inhabited by the memories of long-dead Martians who had eked out pitiful lifespans in harsh conditions.

She hadn't anticipated returning to her original home, yet if she were to ever find out more about her origins, now was her chance. Until she spoke with Ozment, she'd never considered that her deceased, anonymous parents might have been underworlders. The records of her birth had been lost in the colony disaster that claimed their lives, but it would have been easy for her to find out her genetic status. Like many things in her painful past, she chose not to dwell on it. She'd chosen to stay out of the whole modded/natural debate.

She just didn't know if she could bring herself to investigate her past. Facing an attack of hostile aliens on a far-flung planet seemed a more inviting option.

An interface embedded on the wall of the hotel room beeped, distracting Jas from her musings. It was the hotel reception. She accepted the call. The receptionist who had checked her in appeared on the screen. Like Jas and all other Martians, his skin was deep olive, and his eyes and hair were reddish-brown.

"Hi. Is your room to your satisfaction, Ms. Harrington?"

"Yes, everything's fine."

"Great. I hope you don't mind, but I just checked your passport details, and I saw that it's been quite a while since you visited Mars?"

"That's right."

"In case you haven't yet read the room information, I thought I would just let you know that the Rad X protocol still applies. Please try to limit your above-ground time. In the event of a solar storm warning, stay underground until further notice. You'll find your bed access to the right of the screen."

"Okay, I've got it."

"Thank you. Our dining room is currently open and

closes at nine. Breakfast starts at seven-thirty. Let us know if there's anything else we can help you with. Enjoy your stay."

The screen turned dark.

Jas had forgotten about the radiation exposure avoidance protocol. All Martians received mandatory gene therapy to help protect them from the sun's radiation. It gave them their unusual coloring, but it only went so far. Exposure to radioactive solar and cosmic particles still increased the risk of cancer over the long term and prolonged exposure could cause radiation sickness.

The hyperloop to the hotel had been above ground, but the journey had taken only around half an hour. She could easily get to Valles Marineris 5 and back within a couple of hours. The question was, did she want to visit the site of her parents' deaths and the largest disaster in the history of human colonization? She didn't have to. She was there to find out what the Transgalactic Council were doing about the Shadows. No one would say anything if she didn't go.

Her mouth went dry at the thought of visiting VM5, though she knew that, realistically, she had nothing to fear. The settlement had no doubt been rebuilt years ago. Not a trace of the devastation would remain. VM5 would consist of the same drab domes and tunnels as the other towns, connecting a few thousand underground homes, shops, workplaces, and factories.

Would it hurt her just to go and see it? Maybe the experience would do her good. All her life she'd been running away from her past. Her long habit had cost her the sense of any place being her home. It had also cost her friends, and now it was looking like it might cost her Carl.

She smiled at the irony of the situation. Her job required her to be the bravest person aboard a starship. She was the one who was expected to walk first into unknown danger. Yet in reality, she was a coward.

Moving swiftly before she lost her resolve, she pressed the interface to call reception for transport information. Though the idea made her legs go weak, she would visit VM5.

THE HYPERLOOP GATE warbled as Jas swiped her card and passed through. In some ways, returning to Mars was like stepping back into the past. Credchip technology hadn't reached the colony. For Jas, this was fortunate as she no longer carried a credchip beneath the skin on the inside of her right wrist. A scar was all that remained from where an underworlder had forcibly removed it, but Phelan had supplied her with ample funds to preload onto a credcard.

The single-carriage hyperloop module arrived within a few minutes. Jas went aboard. She had her choice of the ten seats in the small, empty carriage. She sat down uneasily, wondering why there were no other passengers. Martian society shared many similarities with Earth's. Weekday evenings were commuter time, and Jas had expected at least some workers returning to VM5 from jobs outside the settlement.

As the module stopped at more stations, a trickle of people got on and off. Jas's only respite from her growing disquiet was the way that she was ignored by the other passengers. She was just another Martian. No one took any notice of her. She'd never quite gotten used to the double takes and sidelong glances her appearance attracted among Earthers.

VM5 was the farthest point on the loop. The carriage

was once more empty when Jas arrived. The doors hissed open and she alighted. It was like being ejected into a scene from a history vid. She was surrounded by plain metal walls, devoid of even the simple, old-fashioned interfaces and their scrolling ads she'd seen at other stations on her journey. The gates were from an earlier era too. The station was deserted.

Dread grew in Jas. Her trip was intended to reassure her that time had moved on, that the colony had been rebuilt and repopulated, and the terrible disaster had been forgotten. The idea had been, as far as she'd formed one, to convince herself that it was time for her to move on too.

She hesitated at the gate. *Krat it.* She wasn't going to run away any more. Setting her jaw, Jas swiped her card. The gate chimed. Even the sound was different from the rest of the hyperloop. She stepped through and left through the only exit.

A few minutes' walk along a bare tunnel that sloped gently down, taking her underground, brought her to a set of closed, plain metal doors and a booth. What was going on? Why was the settlement shut up? Where was everyone?

An attendant was in the process of closing down the booth. He stopped what he was doing at Jas's approach and glanced at his screen. "Sorry, closing in five minutes. Not a lot of point going in now. Maybe come back tomorrow?"

Jas stood before the man, her hands gripping the edge of his desk. He looked from her hands to her face. His expression took on the appearance of mild alarm. "Er...it's five minutes until—"

"I heard you." Jas's mind was whirring so much she struggled to know what to say. "I just need to...could you help me?"

The man's alarmed look deepened. "Are you feeling all

right? Maybe you should sit down?" He moved aside to offer her his chair.

"I'm okay. I just need to know..." Jas's grip tightened. "What's going on? Where are the inhabitants? And why's everything so outdated?"

"Oh." The man's features relaxed. "I think you're a bit confused. This is Valles Marineris Five, the scene of a colony disaster. If you go back to the Loop, it'll take you where—"

"I *know* this is VM5. What I don't know...wait." Everything began to slot into place. The old-fashioned station and tunnel, the attendant in his booth. "Is this some kind of museum?"

"Yes, that's right," the man said, as if he were talking to a five year old. "No need for any alarm. Just head back to the—"

"No. I'm where I want to be. I meant to come here. It's just that I wasn't expecting this. Didn't they rebuild after the disaster?" She tried to remember back to her time in the Martian institute for cared-for children. She couldn't recall anyone telling her what happened to VM5. No one had told her it was being turned into an attraction.

"No, VM5 was never rebuilt. I'm surprised you don't know that. Have you been away from Mars for a long time? No, they made the place safe and it stayed as it was for a few years. But no one was willing to invest in repair and renovation. It was cheaper to excavate another settlement. As time went on, there were calls to demolish it. Raze the site. Then finally they put it to a vote, and the Territory elected to preserve it in memory of those who'd died and as a warning to future generations about what could happen if they don't put safety first.

"But," said the man, swiping his interface closed and

putting on his coat, "VM5's closed right now. You can take a tour tomorrow, if you come back."

Jas looked at the closed doors at the entrance to VM5, then back at the man. The shock of finding her birthplace hardly touched since her parents' deaths was dissipating a little. It was being replaced by a compulsion to go through those doors. The feeling was so strong that she was nauseated. She knew that if she left, she might never find the courage to return.

"I want to go inside. Now. I can't come back."

"I'm very sorry," said the attendant. "We're definitely closed. VM5 opens at ten tomorrow and every day except Sunday. You're welcome to return during opening hours and take a tour."

Jas didn't move.

After a moment, the man left and walked a short distance up the tunnel.

Jas still didn't move. "Please?" she said to the departing man's back.

He stopped and turned. He tilted his head. "It really means that much to you? Can I ask why it's so important that you see VM5 right now?"

Jas glanced back at the closed doors once more. She swallowed. "I was born somewhere in there. My parents died in the disaster, but I survived and...I...just...need to go in."

8

Sparks's transition from scientist to guinea pig had been abrupt. After what had felt like an eternity of bliss, he woke up in a hospital bed within the research facility. At first, the quiet, regular beeps and flickering glow of lights on the monitoring equipment were confused with the serene vision passing through his mind. He thought the sounds and lights were only another manifestation of the perfect beauty and splendor he'd seen since trying to take a scalpel to the Paths. As more and more of his dream faded, the terrible realization that it was all ending hit him.

A ceiling came into focus high above, and Sparks gradually became aware that his mouth and throat were very dry. He worked his tongue and lips, trying to generate some moisture. He moved, weakly, and discovered that plastic tubes had been inserted into him to supply water and nutrients and to drain his waste.

He closed his eyes and tried to will himself back to the place he'd left. It had felt like an actual place that he'd been in, not a dream, even though he had the evidence of his physical body being on a hospital bed. If only he could slip back into a coma, maybe he wouldn't ever have to leave that wonderful place again.

It was no good. The last threads of paradise broke and scattered, and Sparks was back in the medical center within the research facility on Mars. Despair overwhelmed him. He groaned out his frustration and unhappiness. The sound of his voice, or perhaps the alterations in his brain waves, blood pressure, or heart rate registered by the monitoring equipment brought a nurse to him.

The man pushed open the door to his room and locked eyes. But before entering, the nurse lifted his lapel to his lips and spoke softly into the comm button pinned there. A professional smile then spread over his face and he completed his entrance.

"Mister Sparks, how are you feeling? It's good to see you awake."

Mister Sparks? He tried to voice his objection to the word, but all that would come out of his mouth was an angry croak. He tried to lift his arms to gesture, but they were so weak that even the light blanket that lay over him restrained them.

"Take it easy," said the nurse. "Take it easy. Everything will feel strange for a little while, until you get your strength back." He went to a monitor, bent down to peer at the screen, and adjusted something. His head turned briefly to the door, as if he were expecting someone.

"Water," Sparks managed to whisper, but the nurse either didn't hear him or was ignoring him. With a great effort, Sparks cleared his throat. "Water," he repeated, louder.

The nurse straightened up and turned to him. "You'd like some water? Sure. Just a sip. Don't want to shock your system." He filled a paper cup from the wall dispenser and pressed something at the bottom of Sparks's bed with his foot. "Coming up," he said, as the bed began to vibrate and the section below the upper half of Sparks's body began to slowly rise.

The nurse held the cup to Sparks's lips. He was taking a small mouthful of water when his fellow researchers arrived. *He* thought of *them* as his fellow researchers, anyway. It wasn't at all clear whether they thought of him in the same way. As they came in, without ringing the chime, their small smiles seemed smiles of satisfaction that they could glean more information from their now-conscious subject, not smiles of relief at his recovery.

"Sparks, you came around. Great," said Rincker. "How are you feeling? You must tell us all about it." He nodded to the nurse, who pressed a screen. They were recording him—recording the results of their experiment.

This attitude from the people he had worked with for the previous few weeks compounded his misery. Where was their respect for a fellow scientist? Where was their gratitude to him for becoming a test subject? Sparks cleared his throat once more. "Must I?"

His question threw the scientists into confusion. They straightened up from their hunched, eager stances over him. A look passed between them.

"Yes, of course you must," said Graydon. "That was the whole point of what you did. Don't you remember?" She said to the others, "Maybe he's suffered some memory loss." She took out the interface she was holding under an arm and tapped at it.

Sparks was determined to cling to the last shred of dignity he had. "My memory is perfectly fine, and I didn't sign any kind of agreement about taking part in this experiment. So unless my understanding of the legislation covering human experimentation is inaccurate, I don't believe I'm under an obligation to tell you anything. I signed nothing. I agreed to nothing. I gave up none of my rights. I could get up right now and walk out of here, and there's nothing any of you could do to stop me."

Though he tried not to show it, he quailed a little as he spoke his final statement. He'd been—he was still—conducting weapons research. He wasn't at all sure that he was as free to leave at any moment as he'd stated. He'd been bluffing, or threatening, or perhaps wishing. He wasn't sure which.

"Oh, come now," said Adrieux. "There's no need for that kind of attitude. We're all in this together, aren't we?"

"Are we?" Sparks asked. "It seems like I'm the one in this bed after having risked my life to carry out an experiment on the Paths, and you three are safe, sound, and healthy, standing around me in your lab coats. It doesn't look to me like we're all in this together."

Rincker pursed his lips and glanced at the others. "Okay, I hear you, Sparks. You just woke up. You aren't in the mood to talk right now. We get it. Let's leave it...a couple of hours? Maybe you'll feel better then."

They left. Sparks was under no illusions about what the man's conciliatory remarks were about. He was still, in their eyes, no longer a colleague but a test subject. Any concern they'd felt toward him as another human being was gone. These were hardened weapons research scientists. It took a certain detachment to do their job effectively, and these three had it in spades. While he'd been a fellow researcher, he'd been a real person to them. Now that he'd become the source of information about a potential weapon, they didn't, or perhaps couldn't, see him in the same light.

"I'll put this here," said the nurse, placing the paper cup on the table next to his bed. "We can begin your recovery program now. It's best to begin it as soon as a patient wakes up. Back in a moment."

The door slid closed behind the nurse. Left to his thoughts, Sparks began to calm down a little. He mentally went over his responses to the scientists. Had he been too hasty in denying their wishes? They were ruthless in their pursuit of results. They would stop at nothing to find out what they wanted to know about the Paths.

A heavy weight settled over him. Had he put his life in danger? If he refused to take part in the research process, what might happen? What did the scientists have the authority to do? Did he already know too much to be allowed to return to his normal duties? The Paths could kill. There was no doubt about that. Would the scientists use him to push them to the limit?

Sparks cursed the day the aliens had been brought aboard the *Galathea*. All his life, he'd done as he was told. How had he ended up like this?

He longed to return to that heavenly place of his coma. Hope flickered within him. The prospect of the Path-induced trance was inviting. If he gave the scientists a little information, he could suggest that he repeat the experiment to find out more. It would be risky, yes, but he knew how far to push the aliens before they reacted. He wouldn't overstep the mark.

At the very least, his plan would buy him time until he could figure a way out of the predicament, and he would return to that wonderful paradise again.

He searched around for the call button and summoned the nurse. The man appeared within seconds. His time seemed to be devoted entirely to Sparks's welfare. Of course it was, Sparks realized. He might now only be a test subject to the other scientists, but he was an extremely important test subject.

"I want to speak to my colleagues," he told the nurse.

After weeks of being ignored and sidelined by Graydon, Rincker and Adrieux, he was going to become an object of their rapt attention. His only hope was to milk the situation for all it was worth.

9

Jas and the attendant at the VM5 entrance waited for his mother. After hearing Jas's story, he'd called her, explaining that she would be very interested in meeting Jas and he was sure that Jas would be interested in meeting her.

The woman couldn't have lived far away, for no more than fifteen minutes after the attendant had finished his call, a short, round figure came bustling down the tunnel. She was late middle-aged. Her nose and chin approached ahead of the rest of her.

She was in a hurry, and she arrived puffing and panting. Leaning on her son's desk, she gripped her side with her other hand as she caught her breath. She repeatedly looked Jas up and down and nodded to herself as she gasped. When she could finally speak, she moved to Jas and shook her hand, clasping it warmly with the other. "Name?" she asked.

"Harrington. Jas Harrington. But I was given my name by the institute where I grew up. I don't know my real name." It felt weird to say it, though it was true. Jas had never really considered that, for a brief time, she'd had a different name. Her *real* name.

"Hmm...Backra Smart," said the woman. "And this is my son, Tony. Did you introduce yourself, Tony?" Before Tony could answer, she went on, "'Course he didn't. Never does. Got no manners. So is it true, what he said? You were born on VM5? And you've come back to see the place after all these years? Well, well, well. Glad you came. So very glad. Please, come inside. Come in. Come in." She went to the doors, but they remained closed. "Tony, open the place up, son."

"But it's..." Tony half-protested before a look from his mother silenced him. He huffed and went to his desk, opened his interface, and keyed in a code. The tunnel was silent but for Backra's continued panting. The click as the lock opened and the swoosh as the doors slid apart were loud.

Backra scurried through in her rolling gait while Jas hung back. Stopping and looking over her shoulder, Backra gestured for Jas to follow. She called to her son, "You wait out there, Tony, in case the inspector comes. The kid would only get in the way," she said softly to Jas as she stepped inside VM5. In spite of her racing heart, Jas suppressed a smile. The *kid* was at least as old as her.

As they went a little farther in, movement-sensitive lighting flickered on. Jas caught her breath. They really had left the place as it had been after the explosion. Jas and Backra stood in a wide lobby, or what remained of a lobby. The walls were entirely black and charred. In places, the heat from the blast had melted the metal, revealing scorched, bare Martian rock.

Noticing Jas's expression, Backra nodded. "It's quite something isn't it? I used to conduct tours, you know, until

Tony took over. Been through the place tens of thousands of times. But you never quite get used to it. What would you like to see?"

"I don't know," Jas replied. "I don't know what there is to see."

"Most visitors are interested in the site of the explosion. What there is left of it, anyway. But I'm guessing you'd like to see the residential areas? They're more interesting in my opinion. Though very sad, of course. Come this way. And tell me all about your connection to VM5. Tony didn't explain it clearly. You were really born here?"

Corridors branched from three sides of the lobby. The remains of signs were just discernible next to the corridor entrance that Backra led Jas to. All she could make out on the carbonized surface were the figures and letters, 6-AE.

"Yes," Jas replied as they set off. Above, lights strung on bare wires looped along the ceiling. "That's what I was told anyway. I've never bothered to dig into my past or check anything out, but I remember when I was young, a carer told me that I'd been born here and that I was the only survivor of the disaster."

"Hmm...maybe I'm imagining it," Backra said, "or maybe my mind's playing tricks now that you've mentioned that, but I think I remember you."

"What?" Jas exclaimed.

"Sorry, dear. I don't mean I knew you as a baby. No. I think I remember hearing that only one person who'd been inside at the time of the explosion survived, and that it was a baby. But I never heard anything official. It wasn't surprising. So much was kept from us about what had happened."

"What do you mean? What was kept from you?"

"Easier to ask what *wasn't* kept from us. I don't think anyone really believed what they said had caused the explosion, for instance. The official explanation didn't make any sense. Oxygen levels beyond safety limits? Electrical fire? Equipment was basic at that time, it's true, but even then we had alarms to tell us if the atmosphere levels went out of balance. We had automatic fire dampeners." Backra sighed and shook her head. "People asked questions, of course. But the more questions were asked, the tighter the Territory Office closed their lips. Wait for the official investigation, they said. Then we'll have answers.

"But the investigation took years, and everyone was busy just struggling to survive. By the time the findings were announced, most people had moved on with their lives. Things were hard enough as it was without embarking on a wild goose chase trying to track down what had really happened. But I could never let it go. Still can't. So it warms my heart, you see, to meet you. To meet someone who made it out alive."

They'd reached a junction, and Backra paused before saying, "This way."

"Can I ask why it means so much to you?" Jas asked. They were passing doors that starkly contrasted with the blackened corridor. They were modern, and they had clearly been placed there to seal away what lay beyond them. Jas hoped they would stop in a moment. It was a lot to take in at once.

"I worked here," said Backra. "My settlement, VM4, was finished, and the VM5 colonists needed some extra help putting on the finishing touches. I'd come over every day to help fit out living quarters and get them ready for new arrivals. They were flooding in at that point. Mars isn't exactly anyone's first choice any more, but at the time it was popular. You could get a ticket to Mars cheaply. Government subsidies. They were glad to see the back of the likes that came here. I liked to meet the new settlers. I liked to hear stories about Earth. I still missed it badly then, even though things weren't good there. Took me quite a while to get used to being a tunnel rat. Don't know if I ever quite made it. Ah. Here we are."

They stopped outside a room. A plaque had been fitted to the wall, simply stating the room's number.

"Only a few rooms are open, but they all look much the same anyway." She opened the door.

It was a simple, two-bedroom apartment, utterly burnt out. Charred furniture remained and blackened lumps that might once have been toys strewed the floor. Though decades had passed since the fire, the smell of burnt metal and plastic still hung faintly in the air. It reminded Jas of the odor of burning defense units, except that it wasn't mixed with the sickening scent of barbecued meat. Thankfully, that smell no longer lingered.

"Do you want to know exactly what happened during the disaster?" Backra asked. "Or would that be too close to the bone?"

"I want to know," Jas replied quickly. Now that she'd taken the first step she wanted to go the whole way and find out all that she could. She *needed* to know.

"Right. Well, stop me if it gets too much." Backra folded her hands together in front of her and began to speak as if reciting from memory. "When the oxygen ignited, fireballs swept down the corridors. They think they were carried on updrafts leading out and into the Loop. Everyone in the open areas was killed instantly. The fireballs ignited everything they touched, and due to the high oxygen levels, a fierce fire quickly started. It consumed the rest of the place within minutes. The high temperatures and volatile gases killed anyone who was still alive after the fireballs passed. If it's any comfort to you, their deaths would have been very quick. I'm sorry."

Jas had a vision of the apartment as it had once been. Very ordinary, but fresh and new. Through an open door leading to a bedroom, she saw a figure holding a small baby. From outside came the sound of a massive explosion. The ground juddered. A mug of coffee on the living room table tottered and fell. The explosion was followed by a deep, soft whoosh as a fireball passed outside. The spilt coffee began to steam. Screams and shrieks followed from outside. The figure hesitated before running to a safety capsule and thrusting the baby inside.

Why didn't the person get in with their baby? Did they think they had time to find the other parent? Did they want to make sure their partner was safe? In Jas's mind, the figure closed the capsule lid. The lock clicked shut. As the person turned and took just one step, a wave of heat overwhelmed them and they fell.

Backra was quietly waiting, giving Jas time for her thoughts.

"You said you can't let go of what happened," Jas said. "Why? Do you think the Territory Office were hiding something? Was there a cover up?"

Backra's mouth drooped sadly. "I knew those people who died, though I didn't work among them long. They were good people. Kind, honest, and brave to come all the way to Mars to make a new life. I couldn't get used to the idea of all those hundreds of lives gone in an instant. Still can't get used to it, even after all these years.

"Was there a cover up? Yes, I'd say there was. There was a lot of foot-dragging that went on, and apart from the general findings of the inquest, the files were sealed. They won't be available to the public for another eighty years.

Anyone who was an adult at the time of the disaster will be dead by then. No one will be around to take the blame. And, like I said, that the fire happened at all is very fishy. If I were to be completely honest with you, I wouldn't be surprised if it was deliberate."

"You think it might have been arson?" Jas asked. "But, why? Why would someone want to kill all those people? That's the act of a monster."

"Because they were underworlders, that's why. Every single blessed one of them. This was before your time. You won't remember, but naturals were hated. I mean really hated. A lot of people thought they were holding back the advancement of the human race. Polluting it with random gene selection. Allowing genetic diseases and weak traits to continue after we finally had the chance to stamp them all out. That was why underworlders ended up in places like this, where they could live their lives in peace. But it wouldn't surprise me if someone had thought they were doing everyone a favor by wiping out a whole load of them at once."

Jas's knees were weak. She wanted to sit down, but there was nowhere for her to sit.

"I'm sorry," Backra said, seeing her expression. "I'm upsetting you with my ramblings. Don't take any notice of me. I'm just an old woman, full of nonsense. Let's go somewhere else. What else would you like to see?"

"I don't think I want to see any more," Jas said. "I think I've seen and heard enough."

10

Jas needed people. She actually needed Carl, but he was hundreds of miles above her somewhere among the unwavering stars in the inky Martian night, and he was probably tired of her and her endless dithering. Strangers would have to do. Voices, color, movement, laughter. She needed all these things.

She was back at the hotel after thanking Backra for her kindness and the stories she'd told. The evening was getting old. She should have gone to bed, but she knew she wouldn't sleep. She wouldn't be able to erase that charred room or Backra's theory on what might have killed all those people, her parents among them, from her mind for a while.

Jas was also getting used to the idea that she was a natural. If everything that she'd been told were true, there didn't seem much doubt about it anymore. She wasn't sure how she felt. She hadn't been disadvantaged. She'd been fairly successful in her life without any modding. Yet she also didn't think she had much in common with underworlders as she knew them. Backra's revelations had left her feeling like she didn't fit in anywhere.

Jas smirked wryly to herself. Same as usual, then.

She called reception. The previous receptionist's shift had finished, and a new face greeted her. "Yes, Ms. Harrington? How can I help you?"

"Can you tell me the closest bar?"

"Certainly. I'll send directions to the closest establishments. Is there anything else I can help you with this evening?"

"No, that's it."

"Great. I'd like to remind you that the hotel's main door is locked at midnight. If you arrive after this time, please contact the night staff via the security panel. Guests are not allowed to invite non-paying guests into their rooms after midnight. Have a good evening."

The receptionist seemed to have an idea about why Jas was going to a bar, but all she wanted was to not be alone.

The Loop conveyed Jas to a bar within fifteen minutes. As she went in, she was relieved when no eyes turned toward her. If she'd done the same thing on Earth, she would have immediately become an object of attention. Here, she was just another lanky, red-haired Martian out for the evening.

The map the receptionist had sent her included seven or eight bars within the vicinity of the hotel. Drinking was a popular pastime on Mars. Buggy racing was another, Jas recalled. Out on the red, rocky, dusty plains, youths would ride their wide-wheeled buggies as far as battery life allowed, and sometimes farther, knowing they wouldn't make it back. Like on most colony worlds, suicide rates among Martians were high, especially among adolescents whose parents couldn't afford to send them to Earth for several years to harden and strengthen their bones. Doomed to life on all-but-lifeless Mars or another low-g planet if they were lucky, many young Martians simply gave up.

Scanning the bar, Jas noticed that a good number of young Martians also sought oblivion in alcohol. She wasn't sure if the drinking age was lower here than on Earth, but some of the bar's patrons were surely below it. The law was a nebulous thing in the colonies.

A human bartender was serving. She wasn't sure if he was there for the personal touch or because Mars was really that far behind the times.

The bar seats were all occupied, but it didn't matter. Though Jas needed people around her, she didn't feel like talking. She took her ordered beer and found a dark corner to sit in. Stretching out her long legs under the small table, she rested her head against the wall behind her and watched the crowd.

The hum of conversation began to take its effect and some of the tension of the last few hours began to ease from her. Jas sipped her beer and tried to mentally tease out the implications of what Backra had told her. Had VM5 been sabotaged to explode? Had all those hundreds of colonists been murdered? Had there been a cover up about it?

Jas didn't know what to do if Backra's suspicions were correct. She didn't have time to deal with a decades-old mystery. If the Shadows weren't in the process of taking over Earth, probably as a prelude to taking over the galaxy, she might have dug further, but as it was, she had more urgent problems to fix. Avenging her long-dead parents would have to wait.

Taking another sip of beer, Jas relaxed a little more. The visit to VM5 had been traumatic, but she was glad she'd gone through with it and seen and heard what she had. For so many years, she'd dreaded the prospect of revisiting her past. It'd seemed to contain too much pain and unhappiness, but, on reflection, seeing VM5 had given her a sense of release. It was as if she'd opened her closet door expecting to see ghosts and monsters but found only dust and cobwebs.

An argument was breaking out at the bar. The bartender was cutting someone off. It was easy to see why. The man could barely hold himself upright on his bar stool. There was something about him that looked odd. Unlike the plainer clothes of the men and women sitting around him, he was wearing a suit.

"I shouldn't have given you your last drink," said the bartender. "That's it. Go home."

"I haven't got a home," slurred the customer.

Jas's beer glass was at her mouth, but she stopped mid-sip. She put down the glass and swallowed the half-mouthful of beer. She knew that voice. She was sure of it.

"No home to go to," continued the drunk man, "'less you count that horrible lil' cubicle at the facility. Nowhere to go. If I go back there, they'll put me in with those things again." He raised his hands as if confessing something shameful. "Not saying I don't like it. I do. But...but..." Sobs began to choke him. "I could *die*. I could *die*. And they don't care. Nobody cares." He slumped onto the bar, his head on his arms. His shoulders began to shake with sobs.

The customers on either side of the man patted him on the back. "Let him sleep it off a bit," one of them said to the bartender. "He isn't doing any harm."

The bartender shook his head like he didn't approve of the idea, but he walked away to serve someone else.

Since the moment Jas had realized who it was, she hadn't taken her eyes off Sparks. She didn't particularly want to reacquaint herself with him, but the odds of seeing him on Mars were so large that she couldn't help watching him. His temporary friends returned to their conversations and failed to notice him slowly slipping from his barstool.

When she realized what was about to happen, she wasn't quick enough to save him. Sparks hit the floor, a misshapen heap of sadness and regret. Jas got to him just after he fell. The disturbance resulted in a brief lull in the buzz. The bartender leaned over the bar to see Jas squatting next to the nearly unconscious man.

"Do you know him?" the bartender asked.

Jas wasn't sure she wanted to take on whatever responsibility an honest response might place on her shoulders, but she nodded, reluctantly.

"Then take him home for me, will ya? Or I'll have to call security."

Even if Jas had known where Sparks lived, she didn't want to take him home. Maybe if she could sober him up a little, he could make his own way back to his place.

"I'll just move him over here if that's okay," she replied. "He isn't that drunk. He's just tired."

The bartender raised his eyebrows. "Yeah, right. Look, I don't care what you do as long as you keep him outta my way and as long as he doesn't puke or piss himself. Okay?"

"Yeah, got it." Jas turned her attention to Sparks. His eyes were open, but he was in a world of his own, mumbling to himself. He was focused on something invisible behind her.

"Sparks," Jas said, "get up." She grabbed him underneath his arms and began hauling him to his feet.

Sparks'ss gaze drifted to her face, and when he saw who she was he started so violently that she almost dropped him. "H-H-Harrington?" His surprise seemed to jolt him out of his drunken stupor. His body grew less floppy and he tried to get his legs underneath him.

"Yes, it's me," Jas said. "Now get on your feet and come with me over here if you don't want to get thrown out."

Sparks made the few steps to her table without too much help. He sat opposite Jas, rested his elbows on the table, and rubbed his face. Some of his slightly haughty demeanor began to return, as if the shame of Jas seeing him in the state he was in hurt his pride. "Harrington. Who'd have thought it?" He smiled ruefully. "I may have had a little too much to drink."

Jas wrinkled her nose, recalling the former physician of the *Galathea's* condescension towards alcoholics and other addicts. "Yeah, I think you may have. What the krat are you doing on Mars?"

11

"Come on, Sis," Phelan pleaded. "It'll be fun. Now that the ore shipment's gone planetside, we can use the hold. We can play in two teams. Right, guys?"

He scanned the faces of everyone sitting at the table in the dining room, his eyes asking for their support. With Jas on Mars, the ship's crew was down to the captain, Sayen, the android navigator, whose name was Prosper, Flahive, and Carl. Prosper was in her cabin. Carl wasn't sure what she did in there, probably recharge or something. Flahive joined them at meals to chat, though he didn't eat human food. Sayen had told Carl that he had a machine in his cabin that cleaned waste from and added nutrients to the liquid in his suit.

Carl wasn't sure that Phelan's transparent attempt to cheer his sister up was such a good idea. She'd been looking a little better since he'd paid her a visit with Flux, but expecting her to take part in some weird new game might be too much.

"What is this game?" Carl asked, easing the pressure on Sayen. "Can you explain it again?"

"It's simple," Phelan replied. "Each team has one person as an attacker and one person as a target. The aim is for the attackers to hit the targets with a ball. Whenever the target's hit, their team gains a point. The side with the most points loses. There are a few more rules, but that's about it."

"So the attackers can get hit without gaining points?" asked Carl.

"That's right. And the targets can *catch* the ball and throw it to their team mate or at the other team's target, but if they get hit, their team gets a point."

"Sounds kind of painful to be the target," said Carl.

"No," Phelan said, waving his hand dismissively. "The ball's pretty big and soft. And it's difficult to throw hard in zero-g."

"Zero-g?"

"Yeah. Did I forget to tell y'all that part? We have to turn off artificial gravity to play. Oh yeah, also you can't touch a surface and hold the ball at the same time."

It did actually sound like a lot of fun, and they'd spent days aboard the ship with nothing to do. Flying the *Bricoleur* using its Oootoon Drive to Mars had been the only interesting thing Carl had done. But Sayen didn't look like she was feeling up to it.

She was bent over her breakfast bowl, her elbow on the table and her chin in her hand while she idly stirred her cereal with a spoon.

"Sayen?" Phelan asked. "What do you think? The bots must have about finished cleaning the hold. I told them to do it over an hour ago. It'll only take me a minute to print the ball."

Sayen lifted her spoon and plopped it in the bowl. “What the hell. Why not?”

“Yes,” Phelan exclaimed. He got up. “Y’all meet me at the hold in half an hour.”

“Print some helmets too,” Sayen called as he was leaving.

“Aww, why?” her brother retorted. “It isn’t that dangerous.”

“From the sound of it, it could be,” Sayen said. “And our visas to go planetside aren’t through yet, so we’d be relying on your sick bay if someone has an accident.”

“My sick bay’s pretty good.”

“If you want me to play, Phelan, print some safety helmets.”

“Okay, Bossypants.”

After Phelan had left, Carl said, “You sure you’re up to it, Sayen? I can say I don’t want to play if it’s too much for you.”

“No, it’s okay. I don’t mind. I want him to stop worrying about me.”

“That’s very wise of you,” said Flahive. “The captain is experiencing strong negative emotions at the moment, somewhat at odds with the impression he’s giving.”

“You probably shouldn’t tell us that,” Carl said.

“I don’t know. He’s only stating the obvious, to me anyway,” Sayen said.

“You, however,” Flahive said, “seem to be feeling a little better.”

“Yes, I think so,” said Sayen.

“Are you going to play?” Carl asked Flahive.

“I’d like to, but my suit is too restricting. I think the captain has Prosper in mind as the fourth player.”

Flahive was right, though Phelan said they needed the alien's services to act as a referee. He'd printed helmets for everyone but Prosper, who didn't need one as her metal/silicon skull was tough enough. Carl hadn't spoken much with the android. She could hold a simple conversation, but that seemed to be as far as her abilities went.

"I think it'll be fairest if me and Carl play against Sayen and Prosper," Phelan said. "Prosper's the strongest and fastest of all of us, so that way we'll be evenly matched."

"You think I need Prosper on my side to stand a chance of beating you two?" Sayen asked, a glint in her eye.

"Come on, Sis, you're easily the weakest of all of us. But with Prosper working with you, it evens everything out. Let her be the attacker, and you be the target."

"I've got a better idea," Sayen said. "You and Prosper against me and Carl."

"Well that doesn't make any sense," Phelan replied. "I've played this before and Prosper could beat any of us with both hands tied behind her back. Together, we'll beat you two easily. It'll be boring."

"Humor me, okay?"

"If you're gonna insist, you can have it your way." Phelan handed out the helmets and closed the hold door.

Carl and Sayen went to the opposite end of the large, square, metal-walled room. Ordinarily, it was used to store the precious metal-bearing ore that Phelan mined.

"Does Phelan know about your enhancements?" Carl asked Sayen quietly as they went.

"No," Sayen replied, a small smile brightening her sad face. "When we were growing up, Phelan always beat me at everything. He never let up or gave me a chance, even though I was younger and a girl. Let me play attacker this round, okay?"

Carl chuckled. "Go for it."

They put on their helmets and after giving a warning, Phelan turned off the gravity. Everyone rose gently upward. Carl and Sayen were at the back wall of the chamber, ready to push off. Flahive was in the middle. Prosper had the ball.

"Go," Phelan shouted. Prosper threw the ball hard at Carl, but Sayen was ready. She caught it, and almost too fast to see, with a flick of her wrist she threw it at Phelan, who was still fastening his helmet strap. Even at the distance across the hold, the look of shock on his face as the ball hit him square in his chest was comical.

"Phelan and Prosper, one point," announced Flahive, his deep voice echoing around the chamber.

"Prosper," complained Phelan. "Pay attention." He hadn't seen the first interaction and lay the blame on the android.

"I was," said Prosper. "The ball was traveling too fast for me to intercept it."

Phelan pushed off from the wall to grab the floating ball and pass it to her. "Loser goes first," he called to Carl and Sayen and whispered something to the android. Prosper nodded and took aim.

She wasn't aiming directly at Carl, her target, but at the ceiling. Almost too late, Carl realized what she was about to do. The ball left the android's hand. He tried to figure out the angle of the ricochet. He nearly made it out of the way, but not quite. The ball was coming straight for him. At the last millisecond, Sayen snatched it before it hit his shoulder.

"Whoa, fast work, Sis," exclaimed Phelan, sounding a little puzzled.

The words had hardly left his lips before the ball bounced off his helmet after flying across the hold in a blur.

"Phelan and Prosper, two points."

"Whaaa...?" said Phelan.

Carl was fighting the urge to laugh. Sayen turned a somersault and pushed off from the ceiling. She hit the floor with her hands and rebounded. "Loser goes first, right?" she called. "What are you waiting for?"

Phelan was floating lazily near the ceiling, his brow creased into a frown. Pushing off with one hand, he grabbed Prosper's arm and pulled her close.

"Hey, no delays," Sayen said. "It's your turn. Hurry up. Look, your target's right here." She pointed at Carl and winked. "Take your best shot."

Phelan gently pushed Prosper down so that she could reach the ball, which had come to rest a few meters away. He was propelled into a spin. Prosper didn't take aim this time. As soon as she took hold of the ball, she threw it all in one smooth motion. It hit the side of the hold, ricocheted across, bounced off the floor, and came flying toward Carl.

Sayen's hands were clasped together in a double fist. She used them like a racket to return the ball. Phelan was still spinning. When he was facing away from them, the ball hit him on the butt, pushing him gently into the wall.

"Phelan and Prosper, three points," intoned Flahive.

Carl couldn't control himself any longer. He roared with laughter and so did Sayen. Their guffaws were multiplied as they echoed around the bare hold walls. Prosper seemed to get the joke, for she smiled, and Flahive's deep chortles provided a bass note to the cacophony.

Phelan took the joke in good humor and laughed a little himself, though he continued to look puzzled.

Suddenly, he held up a hand. "Hey, guys," he called. "Can it for a minute. A comm's come through."

As the laughter died down, the warble of the interface screen next to the door could be heard. Phelan pushed off from the ceiling and hung upside down at the screen as he accepted the message.

“It’s Jas,” he said. “She says she hasn’t found out anything about Shadows or the Council, but she’s stumbled across something else. Do you guys know anything about aliens called Paths?”

12

Their visas came through the next day, and Carl, Sayen, and Flahive went planetside to meet Jas, Sparks, and the weapons researchers, leaving Phelan and Prosper to look after the ship. Flahive's companionship was desired by all concerned. The scientists at the research institute were especially pleased to hear that an empath was at hand to communicate with the Paths and perhaps shed some light on them. Flahive, too, was interested to talk to the aliens. He didn't recall hearing of them before and wanted to find out all about them.

Carl landed the shuttle at the spaceport and waited until Sayen and Flahive had disembarked before moving it into the hangar. He then went to join them at immigration control. The health check was thorough and included passing through a device that he was sure was a Shadow scanner.

His gaze quickly zoomed in on Jas's tall, shapely figure waiting for them at the gate. She was a welcome sight to his eyes, even after just a couple of days apart. The strength of the hug she gave him after they stepped into Mars Territory lent him some hope for the future.

"Great to see you," she said, "but let's get you below ground quickly. Have you got your Rad X counters?"

Carl held up his arm. After passing the health check, an immigration official had stuck a square of plastic to the inside of his forearm. It was a set of bars that would change color to signal radiation exposure. Currently, the lowest bar was green, and the one above it was pale yellow. The official had told him that if the top bar turned red, he needed to get underground and then to a hospital immediately for radiation treatment.

"Good. You should all be fine. There aren't any solar storms forecast, but it doesn't hurt to be careful. Let's go." She led them to the Loop station, where they caught a train to the research facility. On the way, she related her chance encounter with Sparks.

"It'll be good to see Doctor Sparks again," Sayen said.

"Will it?" Jas asked. "I never understood why you liked him so much."

"He's a great doctor," Sayen replied.

"If you were one of the elite, maybe," said Jas. "He was a misborn to the regular crew."

"That's a little harsh, Jas," Sayen protested. "He had a wonderful bedside manner. He was never in a hurry. He always listened."

"Huh, you never saw his bad side," Jas said. "Anyway, he's changed. You'll see."

When Sparks met them at the research institute reception, Carl saw what Jas meant. The doctor was thin, and though it had only been a few months since they'd last seen him, he looked noticeably older. What was more he had a haunted or hunted, air about him. One of the two. His grin as he greeted them was ghastly.

"Sayen, how pleasant to see you again," Sparks said. "And Carl. And you must be Mr. Flahive. I'm very pleased to make your acquaintance. Step this way, please, everyone. My colleagues are very keen to meet you." He'd brought security clearances for them, which he gave out as they passed inside.

"Have you been studying the Paths ever since we got back from the Polestar mission?" Sayen asked him.

"I have. First aboard a quarantine satellite and latterly here, after an unfortunate accident prompted the removal of the Paths to a more secure setting."

"An unfortunate accident?" asked Flahive.

His booming voice took Sparks by surprise, and he hesitated before answering, "Yes. Our alien friends induced a coma in a technician, and soon after that incident they killed an unauthorized person who entered their chamber."

"They killed someone?" exclaimed Jas. "You didn't tell me that. Flahive, maybe you should reconsider your offer to help."

"Oh, there's no need," Sparks said. "They're quite safe. They only kill when they're under severe threat. Communicating with them telepathically shouldn't cause any harm. I have to confess, I was extremely relieved to hear of your acquaintance, Mr. Flahive. I have high hopes that you may offer the breakthrough we've been looking for all this time."

"I can't promise anything," Flahive replied as he thumped alongside them, "but I'll certainly try my best to help. I believe we're getting close to the creatures? I'm picking up some strong mind waves."

"Excellent," Sparks said. "Excellent. Yes, we're nearly there."

At the end of the corridor, three people in lab coats hovered. As they approached the scientists, a lank-haired one came forward, holding an interface. Though Carl possessed zero telepathic ability, he sensed a great dislike between Sparks and the scientist.

Ignoring the humans, the woman went directly to Flahive. Without any ceremony, she said, "You're the empath, Flahive?"

"Yes," he replied a little late, as if he were concentrating on something else.

"I need you to read through this document and sign it. You have to understand, our work here is top secret. You can't repeat a thing of what we're about to tell you, nor anything that you learn or see involving these creatures."

"Please let me see your document," Flahive said. He manipulated the interface in his flexible disc appendages. The English words disappeared and were replaced by his own written language of spots and splashes. "I'm sorry, this may take me some time to read."

Flahive bent his face plate over the screen and very slowly scrolled down. They waited. The woman scientist looked back at her colleagues, who were impatiently fidgeting at the entrance to the room that presumably held the Paths.

Carl was interested to see the unusual aliens again, though he didn't want to get too close, remembering the powerful emotions that they emanated. Everyone who got within their range of influence was affected. They seemed to be far enough away at the moment as he wasn't feeling anything unusual.

Flahive moved the document down another couple of centimeters. Carl marveled at how slowly he read. Everyone was getting bored standing around with nothing to do. Carl pulled out his personal interface and opened the screen.

"I'm afraid your device won't work in here," Sparks said. "The facility broadcasts a dampening field. For security."

Sighing, Carl slid his interface back into his pocket.

"It's all the same as you would expect," the woman scientist said to Flahive in a blatant effort to hurry him. "I can read it out to you if you'd like."

"Just a little while longer," said Flahive. "I've nearly finished."

But he hadn't nearly finished at all. They stood and waited for at least another ten minutes by Carl's estimation, though it was hard to tell now that his interface wasn't working. Sayen yawned and leaned against the wall. Jas folded her arms and tapped her foot. The woman scientist rolled her eyes at her colleagues.

Finally, Flahive was finished. He shifted the document back into English and returned the interface to the scientist.

"You have to sign it here," she said, holding it back out to him.

"I'm very sorry," Flahive said. "After reading through the terms and restrictions you wish me to agree to, I've decided I'm not prepared to go ahead with communicating with these creatures."

"What?" spluttered Sparks. "But...you have to. He has to, doesn't he?" he asked the woman, a childish whine creeping into his voice.

The scientist was glaring at Flahive. "No, not strictly speaking, he doesn't. If you'll wait a moment, I'll talk with my colleagues. Maybe we can ease some of these requirements. I'll see what we can do."

"No need," said Flahive. "I've changed my mind. I'm no

longer interested in going ahead with this project. Could someone show me the way out?"

"Wait a minute," said Jas. "Are you sure? The Paths...I found them in a significant place. Maybe you can find out something important for us."

"Maybe I could have, but I'm afraid that isn't to be. I'm leaving now. Is the exit this way?"

No matter what anyone said, Flahive wouldn't deviate from his abrupt change of mind. With an air of anti-climax, Carl, Jas, and Sayen left the research facility with the empath.

"Are you sure you won't change your mind?" Sayen asked when Sparks had sadly said goodbye and they were outside. "What did you object to in the document? They seemed prepared to negotiate. Maybe we could go back tomorrow."

Flahive paused and turned back to the facility. He waited until Sparks had gone inside and the doors were closed. "There won't be any need to return. Not to talk with the Paths at any rate. A remarkable species. We had an interesting conversation as I was pretending to read that ridiculous agreement. I believe I may be able to shed some light on these Shadows, and the Paths, and what's been happening both here and in their universe."

13

Jas took them to the bar where she'd met Sparks so they could talk. It was, as she'd predicted, nearly empty. It wasn't yet lunchtime. A few regular patrons were dotted around the place, sitting separately, their heads down and their minds on their beer and inner thoughts. Mars was a place of regrets and unfulfilled dreams, it seemed to Jas. How many had nursed hopes of a better life, only to find themselves trapped on a dry, barren world? A world that attracted no investment now that cheaper interstellar travel had opened the gateway to planets that offered richer, more easily exploited resources?

The bartender was cleaning the bar when they went in. He paused and did a double take at Flahive in his high-pressure suit and smoky face panel, but after a moment he continued wiping. Jas ordered everyone but Flahive a drink.

"Your friend not joining you today?" he asked as he made the drinks.

"You mean that guy I helped last night?" Jas asked in return. "No, he's working. And he isn't my friend."

"Right. Well, thanks for lending a hand with him." He

put a full glass down on the bar in front of Jas. "I don't mind the regular drunks; it's the noisy, falling down drunks I don't like."

"Sorry about that, but, like I said, he isn't my friend."

"Whatever you say." The bartender put down another full glass. When the order was filled, Jas handed over her card. As he gave it back, the bartender didn't let go as Jas took it, so they were both holding it. "I get off at two. If you fancy going for a late lunch, meet me outside." He released Jas's card.

She couldn't help but smile to herself as she took the drinks to the table where the others were waiting.

"Something funny?" Sayen asked.

"The bartender just asked me out on a date," Jas replied as she gave everyone their drinks.

"Ha," Sayen chuckled. "That's nice and flattering. Did you tell him you can't accept because you're on a mission to save the galaxy?"

"Huh, no," Jas said. "It was more strange than flattering. I'm not used to being asked out. I'm more used to negative attention. I keep forgetting that here I'm normal."

"Maybe we could get on to what Flahive wants to tell us," Carl said edgily.

Jas sat down.

"I'm not sure where to begin," Flahive said. His deep voice boomed around the bar, causing heads to turn. He seemed to do something to his translator, for the next time he spoke it was at half the former volume. "I think it's best if I begin by asking you a question. Where did you first encounter the Paths?"

Jas explained how she'd found them deep within a Shadow trap and, under Haggardy's orders, transported them to the *Galathea* as a new resource for Polestar. She also explained how they'd ended up on Mars, according to Sparks.

"Their initial location makes a lot of sense to me," Flahive said, "based on what the Paths said."

"So you can talk to them?" Jas asked. "We only pick up on their emotions."

"I can converse with them," Flahive replied. "And when you say you pick up on their emotions, you should understand that they also pick up on yours. The best way to describe the phenomenon you humans quaintly refer to as telepathy or mind-reading is that feelings and thoughts are like music and lyrics. The analogy is accurate in that distance is inversely related to the strength of the signal received, and also in that the music of a song—the emotions—are easier to make out than the lyrics—the thoughts. Unfortunately for humans, you're all but deaf when it comes to perceiving emotions and thoughts, though you do transmit rather loudly."

Carl asked, "So how come we feel what the Paths feel?"

"On this plane," Flahive replied, "the Paths are extremely handicapped except for their—for want of a better word—telepathy. Their signal is even louder than a human being's. So loud, in fact, it's equivalent to them shouting at the tops of their voices. Hearing them was almost painful. I had to ask them to whisper."

"Wait," Sayen said. "What do you mean, *on this plane*?"

"I mean in this dimension. The Paths are from another, um, *place*. Another universe, I think, or perhaps something different from a universe. It's all a little confusing to me, even after talking with them for some time. I'll explain it as well as I can, then please feel free to ask me any questions. I may not remember it all perfectly. I couldn't write anything down under the scrutiny of the scientists."

Flahive settled in his seat. He took up a whole bench, and, as always, he looked uncomfortable. His third leg stuck out at the front, which prevented him from sitting close to the table.

"The Paths are from a place that has no physical structure. According to the known laws of physics, it doesn't exist. This place has no atomic particles, no forces, no time, nothing. I'm not sure if the word *place* even applies. I'm afraid the Paths didn't seem to have words to describe their home. They could only tell me about it in terms of what it *isn't*, not what it *is*, because even language doesn't exist or have any meaning there.

"The next thing they told me may be the crucial key to understanding and defeating the aliens you call Shadows. The Paths said that Shadows also come from this place that isn't a place. They create traps in our universe so that they can cross over. They absorb their victims, including their brains, which hold their memories and personality, and recreate that person, only with a Shadow mind. The Paths said that the Shadows are all one thing, but also many things together. They also said that they're aware of what the Shadows are doing, and they're trying to stop them, but here in the physical world, they're nearly helpless.

"They didn't actually tell me this," Flahive went on, "but from what you've said, the Paths appeared in the Shadow trap because they wanted to fight the Shadows or try to warn their victims. Or it may have been because that was where it was easiest for them to pass through. I'm not sure."

"Whoa," said Carl.

"I thought I might find you all here," said a voice. "Do you mind if I join you?" They'd been so intent on what Flahive was saying, no one had noticed that Sparks had come in.

Jas wondered how much he'd heard.

Sparks didn't wait for an answer. He pulled up a chair and sat down.

"Doctor Sparks," Sayen said. "Did you hear what Flahive was saying about the Paths? They're fighting the Shadows too."

Jas shook her head at her.

"Oh, come on, Jas," Sayen said. "We're all on the same side, aren't we?"

"No," Jas said, "I don't think we are."

"You're right, in a way, Harrington," Sparks said. "However, *I'm* not your enemy." He turned to Flahive. "Am I right in understanding that you were pretending to read that agreement while, in fact, you were speaking to the Paths?"

Flahive didn't answer, possibly waiting for an indication from one of the others as to whether or not he should tell Sparks what he knew.

"Carl, what do you think?" Jas asked.

He shrugged. "I don't know. He's working with the research team. I don't know whose side he's on."

"He's on the side of humankind," Sayen said. "We all are. We should go back to the research facility and tell them what Flahive found out."

"I wouldn't advise that," Flahive said. "I don't think those humans who have been working with the Paths are very good people." He didn't say more, but it was evident that that was the reason he'd indulged in subterfuge. The Paths must have told him something that caused him to distrust the scientists.

"They aren't good people," Sparks exclaimed so vehemently it made the others jump. "They are *not* good people. That's why I came here to find you. I wanted to ask you if you could help me get away from here."

Sparks proceeded to spout a torrent of words explaining his experiences over the last months and what the other scientists had been forcing him to do. From what she could gather, Jas concluded that the doctor had been turned from a researcher into a lab rat.

"The coma experience is pleasant enough while it lasts, I confess," Sparks said, "but the Paths are capable of killing. They killed a member of staff on the quarantine station. They've killed animals that we set on them. I just know that those misborn colleagues of mine are going to push me to take more and more risks until the Paths kill me too. And then they'll dissect me like they did all the other animals."

Sayen's eyes had grown round. "Jas, Carl, we have to do something."

"Why don't you just quit?" Jas asked.

"I can't," Sparks replied. "I've tried. Yesterday, when you met me here, I'd been to the spaceport. I had all my things packed. I was ready to give up my job, everything. I was ready to return to Earth with little more than the clothes on my back and start again. But I was stopped from boarding the shuttle. *Travel permission denied*, they said. Since when did we need permission to travel? And where could I flee to on Mars? Where could I hide? They'd find me in a second. Please, could you smuggle me aboard your shuttle, Lingiari? I'll pay you anything."

"You didn't tell me this," Jas said. "You told me you'd been working with the Paths. That was all."

Sparks replied, "I was hoping I had my ticket out when you said you knew someone who could help with understanding the Paths, Harrington. I thought if we had a breakthrough in our experiments, it would take the pressure off and I'd be allowed to leave. When your friend refused to help, I despaired. That's why I came to find you. I wanted to persuade him to reconsider."

"Okay, okay. So you can't leave, but wait a minute," Jas said. "Back up. What did you mean when you said, *the coma's pleasant enough while it lasts*?"

With so much for them to talk about, the group remained at the bar until the evening.

14

"What? No," Phelan said. "I'm not risking my shuttle...I'm not risking my ship...on anything so hare-brained."

"You have to," said Sayen. "The Paths could be the key to defeating the Shadows. They could be the key to everything that's been happening. We need to get them out of that facility. Then Flahive can talk to them. They could hold vital information. They're our link to the dimension where the Shadows come from. We can't leave them down there in the hands of those weapons scientists."

Jas, Carl, Flahive, and Sayen had joined Phelan on the bridge of the *Bricoleur* after leaving Sparks on Mars with a promise that they would consider his request for help.

"Sis, this isn't like rescuing you from the roof of a burning building," said Phelan. He threw his baseball at the ceiling and caught it. "Mars has defenses. If we swoop into their airspace without clearance, they'll shoot us out of the sky."

"We've got clearance, mate," Carl said. "I've been planetside three times. It won't look unusual if I take the shuttle down again."

"So you're going to land at the spaceport?" Phelan asked. *Thunk.* He sighed. "Okay, tell me your plan."

Sayen grinned. "With Sparks's help, we break the Paths out of the research facility, take them aboard the shuttle, and bring them up here. Then jump somewhere. Quickly."

"Just like that, huh?" said Phelan. "You're gonna break into a top-security facility, steal highly classified experiment subjects, *somehow* get them through export screening at the spaceport, and bring them up here?"

Sayen nodded. "That's the plan."

"Seriously?" *Thunk.*

"We'll have to do it really fast."

"You're certainly a lot faster than I remember you being, Sis, but I don't think being fast is going to cut it this time."

"Phelan," Jas said, "I understand your reluctance, but ever since we found the Shadows, we've had to take risks. We've risked our lives I don't know how many times. Believe me, I'd rather face Martian security and a handful of mad scientists than Shadows."

Phelan remained indecisive. He threw his baseball.

Sayen leapt into the air and caught it before it reached the ceiling. "*I* don't understand your reluctance," she said as she hit the ground. "You don't sound like the Phelan I know, who ran away to space at eighteen, or the man who makes his living mining uncharted planets on the Outer Rim. What's the problem, Brother? I don't get it."

Phelan looked intently at Sayen, and for a moment the confident, carefree mask fell away. In its place was the look of a man who loved his sister very much and couldn't bear the thought of losing her, the last family he had.

Wordlessly, Sayen tossed him his baseball and went over and hugged him.

Jas thought she heard Flahive give a small sigh of contentment. She supposed there was an upside to picking up on the emotions of others.

"Captain," Flahive said, "though this proposal is risky and the consequences of our capture are unknown, I believe we should make the effort. In the short time that I had to speak to the Paths, it became clear to me that these creatures are of great importance not only in defeating the Shadows, but also in helping us understand the nature of their universe. It's little short of a crime that they've been shut away and experimented upon. To try to use their special ability as a weapon is immoral. It's deplorable, in fact. The Paths are suffering, and we have a duty to rescue them."

Phelan said, "I hear what you're saying, Flahive, but I'm also wary of bringing these creatures aboard my ship if they're killers, as everyone's saying."

"I think I may be able to shed some light on that also," Flahive replied. "Doctor Sparks was saying that he enters a kind of trance or coma when he does something to threaten the Paths, and that they kill any living thing that might cause them serious harm. I didn't discuss this reaction with the Paths as I wasn't aware of it at the time that I spoke with them, but if I had to guess, I'd say that they aren't intentionally killing their victims. I believe that the Paths' only defense is their access to the dimension where they usually live. I believe they are stopping their victims' actions by sending them temporarily or permanently into their own dimension."

"Krat," Jas said. "You could be right. It's about the only

power they have here. It's the only thing they can do to help themselves."

"So are you saying," Phelan asked, "that as long as they don't feel threatened, they won't hurt us?"

"I'm confident of it," Flahive replied. "If I'm here to translate for them, they'll trust us. No one will come to any harm."

Phelan sighed and rubbed his forehead. "I think I'm probably gonna regret this, but okay. Okay. Y'all can go and get these Paths and bring them aboard my ship, though where we'll go after that, I've no idea."

"Thanks, Phelan," Sayen said, giving him another hug.

"Whoa, hey Sis, those are some powerful arms you've got yourself there. Ease up a little."

"Sorry." Sayen released Phelan and turned to the others. "When are we going to do it?"

"No time like the present," Jas said. "How about tonight?"

15

Phelan had provided an encrypted comm line to make the arrangements with Sparks. The doctor would meet them at the entrance to the research facility at ten o'clock, when everyone but the security staff would have left. Sparks would say he was working late. Though his status had dropped in the eyes of his colleagues, he retained the necessary clearances to admit guests into the building.

The plan for how they would get the Paths out of the facility was a little fuzzy. They would have to get them past the security guards. How they would do that was unclear. Phelan had the standard complement of weapons you would expect to find on a starship that regularly trawled lawless parts of the galaxy, but there was no way they would get them through customs. Even to try would arouse suspicion. They would be going in empty-handed and would have to rely on speed, bravado, and a lot of luck to see them through.

How they would convince the spaceport officials to allow them to take the Paths aboard the shuttle was another unanswered question. They would have to cross both those bridges when they came to them, Jas concluded as she strapped herself into her shuttle seat, ready to make the descent to the Valles Marineris Spaceport. Things were going to get worse, not better, for the Paths. This would be the best chance they had to rescue them. They had to take it.

Flahive was a concern. Jas had thought that, coming from a high-g planet, he would be fast and strong in Mars' low gravity, but his awkward method of locomotion made him slow. She wondered if his species was aquatic and so walking on land was unnatural to him. His presence was essential, however, if they were to reassure the Paths that they meant them no harm and if they were to avoid the potentially deadly consequences of scaring them.

She was pleased to have Sayen along. Her super speed, strength, and imperviousness to heat and cold made her a valuable team member in any raid. Carl would remain with the shuttle in case they needed to make a quick getaway. They had button comm links to stay in touch.

With Sparks, they had four people to bring the Paths to the spaceport. They should be able to manage it, Jas guessed. If she recalled correctly, the creatures were waist high and half as wide, but they were hollow and light to carry. She hoped the emotions they would emanate as they were being taken away would be positive ones.

"Touchdown in five," came Carl's Australian drawl over the cabin speaker. Jas wished she'd had more time to talk to him since visiting VM5. Delving into her past on Mars had been less painful and more cathartic than she'd imagined. She felt she'd gathered a little courage, maybe enough to acknowledge her feelings about him.

The shuttle landed, and fifteen minutes later they were through all the checks and on their way to the research facility. Sparks met them at the door, his manner very calm and professional. Jas marveled at his acting ability. He had to be nervous and worried, but he didn't show it. Then she recalled how Sayen would rave about his skills as a physician. The man had had long years of practice exuding an aura of confidence.

"Thank you so much for reconsidering your decision," Sparks said as he ushered them in. When a security guard approached, frowning suspiciously, he told the man, "You remember our guests from yesterday? They're paying us a return visit. No cause for alarm."

Ignoring the guard's unconvinced look, he swept them over to the unstaffed reception desk. "We have to go through the formalities, of course. Let me check you in." He tapped at a screen and handed them temporary security passes. They went through the secure inner entrance.

So far, so good, thought Jas.

"As soon as I'm within range, I'll explain to the Paths why we're here," Flahive said. "They should be fully prepared for our appearance and not alarmed."

"Great," Jas said, scanning the surroundings for signs of activity. The place seemed to be as Sparks had predicted it would be: utterly deserted. She couldn't hear anything but the sounds of their footfalls and Flahive's soft *bump, thump, bump, thump*.

In a few minutes they were back where they'd been the previous day, at the junction that led to the Paths' confinement chamber. Sparks's scientist colleagues had gone home, however, and the corridor was dim and silent. The doctor approached a wide door with a security panel at eye height to one side of it. He looked into the panel and pressed a button. An almost inaudible click signaled the opening of the lock.

Inside, looking exactly as they had when Jas had first seen them in the Shadow trap, were the Paths. Their odd, inverted bag shapes were just as incongruous as they had been then. She became aware of a sense of great calm and happiness. The Paths were radiating their emotions. Flahive must have done a good job of explaining what they were going to do.

Lifting the Paths was like picking up elongated, suede balloons, though they weren't rigid. The creatures were soft, velvety, and light. They partially collapsed wherever they were held, which was fortunate. It meant that they could carry all of them without too much difficulty.

Their arms full of Paths, they made their way down the corridor toward the exit. Everything had gone smoothly up until then, but that was the easy part. The hard part was going to be getting the Paths past security and then onto the shuttle.

"Do you know what we can say to the guards?" Jas asked Sparks.

"I've no idea," he replied. "I've wracked my brains, but I can't think of a single reason that would justify myself and three strangers removing experimental organisms from the facility. I was hoping you might think of something."

"Krat," Jas said. "We can't fight them. We don't have any weapons, and I don't want anyone to get hurt. But if they see what we're doing of course they'll try to stop us. We'll have to distract them. Is there something you can do to set off an alarm? If they aren't well-trained, they'll both leave their posts to investigate."

"Hmm, good idea," Sparks said. "I think I might be able to manage something."

"Hurry up," Jas said. "We're nearly at the entrance."

Sparks was glancing around as if looking for something.

He said to Flahive, "Could you ask the Paths if one of them would mind if I used them as a water receptacle? Just for a short time."

Flahive was silent for a moment, then replied, "They say that wouldn't be a problem."

"Excellent," Sparks said and disappeared with his Path into a restroom. The sound of running water came from the room, and Sparks reappeared, carrying an inverted Path that was now heavy and round with water. "Could one of you open that, please?" he asked, nodding toward a door on the opposite side of the corridor.

Sayen pushed the door open. Inside the room were ranks of interface screens. It was some kind of classroom or study room. Sparks took a few quick steps and upended the Path over the screens, sending a torrent of water over the electronic equipment. It did the trick. A whooping alarm sounded, and the corridor lights flashed.

"In here," called Sparks, carrying his now-deflated, soggy Path into another empty room.

When they were all inside, Jas held the door open a tiny crack. They waited. After a few moments, a security guard ran past and into the room Sparks had flooded. Just one security guard. *Krat.* The other one must have stayed at his post at the entrance. She had one more ace up her sleeve. She would have to play it. "Run for the entrance, everyone," she said quietly. "Sayen, don't get too far ahead of us. When we're in sight of the guard, let me go first."

They sprinted the final few tens of meters to the lobby and burst through the door. Sayen stepped to one side and let Jas go past. One guard stood at the entrance. As they appeared, he turned and gaped. Jas screamed like a banshee and bore down on him.

The sight and sound of the tall, shrieking Martian

carrying a weird alien and flying toward him made the guard's eyes grow round and his mouth gape. His hand went to his weapon, but he fumbled it. In the second of extra time it took for him to get over his surprise, Jas was on him. A quick, well-placed punch knocked him out cold. A moment later, they were past the unconscious guard and out in the street.

"Run," shouted Jas.

16

Flahive's *bump thump, bump thump* was growing fainter. Jas turned and saw the alien was falling behind. He was too slow. The tunnel they were running down was long and straight, and the guard Jas had knocked out would be coming around within a few seconds. They had to get out of his line of fire.

Telling the others not to wait, and that they would meet them outside the spaceport, she dropped back.

“Please, take my Path and continue without me,” Flahive said. His translator didn't convey the strenuous effort he was making, but his leaps were growing shorter and his legs were wobbling.

“No,” Jas said. “You can make it. Let me help you.” She wrapped an arm awkwardly around his wide frame under his three upper limbs.

“Here,” said Flahive, trying to pass her the alien he was carrying.

“I'm not taking it,” exclaimed Jas. “You can do it. Come on.” She pulled him along another few steps.

"It is too late," said Flahive. He slid from her grip and collapsed.

Jas hadn't heard the laser shot, but as Flahive hit the ground, she saw the damage. A hole had been burned in the back of the empath's pressure suit. A white, wet mass was bulging from the hole, which grew rapidly wider.

"No," yelled Jas.

With the last of his strength, as his body forced its way out of his splitting suit, Flahive lifted the Path he was carrying, holding it up for Jas to take from him. Something fizzed passed her ear. She was being shot at. In the distance, two guards were leaving the open entrance to the research facility. The unconscious guard had woken up and the other had returned from investigating Sparks's distraction. Both were firing at them.

She grabbed the Path from Flahive. A low groan came from the alien's translator. His suit split from top to bottom down the back, and a jelly-like, partially translucent mound erupted like foam from a shaken bottle of soda.

"I have asked...them...to help," were Flahive's dying words.

Holding Paths under each arm, Jas fled, shielded from the guards' sight by Flahive's remains.

Sayen and Sparks were waiting for her just outside the spaceport. Their alien baggage was attracting considerable attention from passersby.

"Where's Flahive?" Sayen asked.

Jas couldn't answer. She could only shake her head. She didn't only have her own grief to deal with. The Paths she was carrying were radiating sadness. She swallowed and said, “We have to get to the shuttle immediately. We have only moments until the guards at the research facility raise the alarm and they close the spaceport.”

“How the heck are we going to explain the Paths?” Sayen asked.

“I’m all out of ideas,” Jas said. “We’ll have to try to bluff our way through.”

“I don’t like this,” Sparks muttered. “I don’t like this at all. I tried to leave once and they wouldn’t let me. My name’s known to them. I was hoping you’d thought of another way.”

“Krat, Sparks,” Jas said angrily. “We’re doing our best. A friend just died. We can’t perform miracles.”

“It *will* be a miracle if we don’t get stopped and arrested,” Sayen said.

“Let’s just try, okay?” said Jas. She couldn’t think straight. She couldn’t shake the image of Flahive’s terrible death from her mind.

They were inside the spaceport and making their way to the security gate. Though they were receiving many curious glances and outright stares, none of the spaceport staff seemed to be aware that they were wanted for stealing highly sensitive potential weapons—yet.

Jas’s heart seemed about to thump its way out of her chest as they neared the gate. The clerk’s face was a picture as she watched them approach. What could they say to her to convince her to let them through? Should they force their way in and make a run for it? It was a couple of hundred meters at least from the security gate to the hangar where Carl was waiting in the shuttle. *Carl.* She’d forgotten to contact him.

Jas lifted her comm button to her lips. “Carl, we’re in the spaceport. Just outside security. We’ve got the Paths.”

"How're you gonna get them to let you through?" he replied.

"Krat knows."

"You can do it, Jas. I'll bring out the shuttle. I'll be waiting for you."

The people in front of them in the line passed through security. As Jas, Sayen, and Sparks stepped up, the clerk put her hands on her hips and raised her eyebrows.

"And what, might I ask, are those?" she asked, staring at the soft, brown aliens they carried.

"Er...they're..." Jas said. Her mind was absolutely blank. She looked at Sayen.

"They're...they're...ornaments," Sayen said. "Souvenirs of our visit."

"Really? Where'd you get them? What are they?" The clerk looked glum as she spoke. The Paths' emotions were affecting her. Jas cursed inwardly. If the clerk was feeling bad, she'd be even less likely to let them into the departure area. When no one seemed able to answer her, she said, "You'll have to take those to the screening office."

"Damnit," Sparks said. "I knew this would happen. I'll never be able to—"

Before he could finish, the clerk's eyes suddenly rolled back in her head, and she fell down in a dead faint. Gasps and exclamations came from the line behind them. For a moment, neither Jas, Sayen, nor Sparks moved. Then Sayen blurted, "It's the Paths. The Paths've put her in a coma."

Hope leaping up within her, Jas shouted, "Let's go," and sped past the unconscious clerk.

Spaceport staff came running up on the other side of security, attracted by the commotion of the crowd. The ones that ventured near the Paths fell like ninepins, creating more confusion.

"Carl," Jas yelled into her comm button, "we're on our way."

Within moments, they were racing down the tunnel that led to the landing pad. *Had Carl gotten permission to take off?*

"Jas," came his voice from her button, "I can't get permission to take off. It's pandemonium in the control room. No one will talk to me. Don't go down the embarkation tunnel. There's another shuttle at the end of it. "

"What? No," exclaimed Jas. "We're nearly there. We've nearly made it. There has to be a way."

"There is," Carl said. "But you've got to go outside."

"We can't. We'll freeze, and we won't be able to breathe. There aren't any atmosphere suits in here."

"It'll be safe. It's only a short distance to the landing pad, and as long as I'm on it, the other shuttle can't take off. You can hold your breath while you run. There'll be an emergency airlock in there somewhere. Go through it, and run to me. I'll have the door open."

"The airlock's here," cried Sayen, who had overheard Carl's words. She was doubling back. "We just ran past it."

Jas reversed, and Sparks was hot on her heels. They skidded to a halt next to Sayen. She was reading the instructions to open the airlock.

"Just smash the emergency button," Jas yelled.

Sayen cracked the glass over the emergency panel and pressed the button. With the harsh, metallic clank of long-unused parts, the airlock opened. They stepped inside, and the door closed, sealing them in. In another moment, Sayen located the button to open the outer door, which would lead them out into Mars' frigid, thin atmosphere.

"Ready?" Sayen asked.

"No," Sparks replied. "I think we should—"

"Hold your breath," said Sayen as she punched the

button. The outer door slid back. Jas fought not to gasp as the icy cold atmosphere swept inside. A short distance away was the familiar sight of the *Bricoleur*'s shuttle. Less than a one-minute run, Jas estimated. She and Sayen could do it. She wasn't so sure about Sparks.

She pointed, and they ran.

Sayen reached the shuttle way ahead of Jas and Sparks. She disappeared into the dark space of the entrance. A moment later, she reappeared without the Paths she'd been carrying and came back to them.

Jas's lungs were screaming at her to breathe. Darkness was blurring the edge of her vision. A thud came from beside her. Sparks had fallen.

But Sayen was there. She picked up the doctor and hoisted him over her shoulder. Jas groped for the dropped Paths. She had them. There were only meters to go. Sayen was already carrying Sparks into the shuttle, her petite frame comically dwarfed by her impossibly large burden.

With the last of her strength, Jas forced her legs to move. In a daze, she took her final steps into the shuttle and crumpled to the floor.

17

Warmth and feeling returned to Jas's extremities as she sat in the passenger cabin and caught her breath. Gradually, the ache in her lungs and throat eased. She was dimly aware of the movement of the shuttle as they went up through the Martian atmosphere and pressure forced her down into her seat. She hadn't even fastened her safety belt.

Carl was flying to the *Bricoleur* faster than he had on the other trips. Were the Martian authorities already on their tail? Jas tried to ease her mind. There wasn't much she could do if that were the case. Their escape was now in Carl's and Phelan's hands.

Sparks sat across the aisle. He was white and trembling. The Paths were immobile, as always, lying where they'd been put, on seats and on the floor. The g-force of the flight was compressing their soft forms. Jas wondered what they were thinking.

Sayen caught her eye and gave her a thumbs up. She smiled back. They couldn't have made it without her. Jas was glad her friend had been able to move on a little from her terrible grief and depression.

After what seemed a long time, the g-force eased. They had to be approaching the *Bricoleur*. The shuttle's vibration calmed, and Jas's stomach pushed against her diaphragm as their motion abruptly slowed. They came to a stop. The clank of the access hatch joining the ship echoed through the cabin.

As the hatch scraped open, Sparks scrambled from his seat. Ignoring the Paths, he ran through the opening and into the *Bricoleur*.

"I'll take these, then?" Sayen asked his departing back. She gathered together as many Paths as she could carry. "Can you bring the rest, Jas?" she asked before she left too.

Jas got up and began to collect the remaining Paths. Carl came in from the pilot's cabin.

"What happened to Flahive?" he asked.

"He got shot by a guard. The burn pierced his suit." Her chin trembled.

Carl looked downcast. "When I saw he wasn't with you, I knew something bad had happened. I thought, I'll have to go without him."

"You did the right thing."

Jas continued to pick up Paths. With Flahive's help, they'd done what they'd set out to do. They'd saved the Paths from experimentation, and now they might be able to use them to defeat the Shadows, though Jas wasn't sure how, now that they had no way to talk to them. She was physically and emotionally exhausted after her brief time on Mars. Yet she was glad they'd gone there.

Carl was watching her. He opened his mouth to speak then seemed to change his mind.

"Were you going to say something?" Jas asked.

"We should go through to the ship. We've got to jump. Mars won't let us get away easily after that little stunt."

"Was that all you were going to say?"

Carl shook his head. "Now's not a good time."

Jas winced at the ache in his eyes. Her heart was in her throat. "Maybe it is."

He looked up, hopeful. "What *is* there to say, Jas? You know how I feel."

"I do." Her pulse was thumping in her ears. "And...I feel the same." She carefully put the Paths down.

Carl moved closer. "You said once, until we get rid of the Shadows, it wasn't a good idea to move ahead with a relationship."

"I did say that."

"But," Carl went on, "isn't that a good reason *not* to delay being with someone? Because we don't know how much time we have left."

He was right. Jas couldn't argue with him, and she didn't want to. But that old dread she felt was rising up in her again. She knew where it came from, and it was something that a trip to Mars couldn't fix. She looked down.

"Jas," Carl said softly. He brought his face close to hers, so that his lips were millimeters from her mouth. But he stopped. He didn't kiss her. He was waiting for her to make the move. She had to decide.

She was frozen. Her feelings for Carl were equally matched by her terror of repeating the emotional devastation she'd experienced once before.

The moment was over. With a barely audible sigh, Carl moved away from her.

Jas couldn't bear it. She couldn't bear to let him go. Before Carl could move out of her reach, she grabbed him and kissed him. He held her close, his hands pressed into the small of her back. She was in his arms, his lips were on hers, and she didn't want the feeling to ever end.

"Guys," someone exclaimed.

With a terrible wrench, Jas and Carl moved apart.

"Sorry, guys." Phelan was standing in the cabin. He'd entered unnoticed by either of them. "We need to jump, now. Mars patrol ships are only ten minutes away."

"Krat," Carl exclaimed and ran out. "Get to your jumpseats, both of you," he shouted behind him as he left.

"Where are we going?" Jas asked Phelan as they ran to the bridge.

"Ganymede."

"Ganymede? Why?"

"That's where the Council told me to go."

"You heard from the Council?"

"A message packet came through while you were on Mars. They traced me through my parents' records. They're going to meet us there. Prosper's plotted the jump, but we need to get out of here fast."

They burst onto the bridge. Carl was already in the pilot's seat. Everyone was strapped in and waiting for them.

"Get in your seats," Carl barked, his hand hovering over the controls. The screen at the front of the deck displayed the surface of Mars. Four patrol ships were in view and growing rapidly larger.

Below them was Valles Marineris, Jas's birthplace, a place she had feared returning to for so long, only to find that the ghosts of her past existed mostly in her head.

They jumped.

JAS'S STORY CONTINUES IN...

SHADOW BATTLE

SHADOWS OF THE VOID BOOK 9

Sign up to my reader group for a free copy of *Starbound*, the Shadows of the Void prequel that tells the story of what happened to Jas Harrington in Antarctica, and for exclusive notice of new releases, advanced reader opportunities and other interesting stuff:

https://jjgreenauthor.com/free-books/

Created with Vellum